The Saga of the Volsungs

with *The Saga of Ragnar Lothbrok*

The Saga of the Volsungs

with *The Saga of Ragnar Lothbrok*

Translated, with Introduction, by

Jackson Crawford

Hackett Publishing Company, Inc.
Indianapolis/Cambridge

For further information, please address
Hackett Publishing Company, Inc.
P.O. Box 44937
Indianapolis, Indiana 46244-0937

www.hackettpublishing.com

Cover design by Brian Rak and Elizabeth L. Wilson
Interior design by Elizabeth L. Wilson
Composition by Aptara, Inc.

Library of Congress Cataloging-in-Publication Data
Names: Crawford, Jackson, translator, editor.
Title: The Saga of the Volsungs : with the Saga of Ragnar Lothbrok /
    translated and edited, with introduction, by Jackson Crawford.
Other titles: Vèolsunga saga. English | Ragnars saga Loᵒbrâokar ok sona hans.
    English.
Description: Indianapolis, Indiana : Hackett Publishing, 2017. | Includes
    bibliographical references.
Identifiers: LCCN 2017008114 | ISBN 9781624666339 (pbk.) | ISBN
    9781624666346 (cloth)
Subjects: LCSH: Sagas—Translations into English.
Classification: LCC PT7287.V7 C73 2017 | DDC 839/.63—dc23
LC record available at https://lccn.loc.gov/2017008114

Contents

To Joe and Candy Turner,
the highest peaks in Wyoming.

Acknowledgments

I am grateful to my students at UC Berkeley, especially Preethi Bhat, Juliana Chia, Adrianna Gabellini, Victoria Glynn, Christopher Hall, Julia Hoyt, Stephan Kaminsky, Boping Kang, Marty Krakora, Dan Laurin, Nahkoura Mahnassi, Heather Newton, Brianna McElrath Panasenco, Joe Shamblin, Scott Shell, Nick Stevens, Matt Willett, Marthe Wold, Peter Woods, Talya Zalipsky, and Wendie Zhang, for reading these translations and providing feedback in the courses in which they were first used. I also thank the two anonymous reviewers for many important suggestions that improved the book on several fronts, and in numerous different ways I am grateful for the kindness and feedback of Thomas Allen, Kathi Brosnan, Adam Carl, Matthew Colville, Michael B. Dougherty, Kate Elliott, Faith Ingwersen, Elizabeth LaVarge-Baptista, Arne Lunde, Bob Maloney, Amanda Minafo, Laet Oliveira, Jordan Phillips, Mark Sandberg, Caley Smith, Rich Stanley, Rosie Taylor, Bob and Barbara Townsend, Moriah VanVleet, Kirsten Wolf, and Reginald Young while this book was being written.

My most heartfelt thanks go to Masha Lepire for her invaluable input on my drafts, to Maths Bertell for many productive discussions about these sagas, to Claire and Travis Crawford for so often throwing a harp into my snake-pit, to Bob and Suzanne Hargis and Remington Bailey for wings and wheels, and to Katherine Crawford, who has often helped me see the vein of silver in translation's ore of words, and who first encouraged me to follow the Poetic Edda with a translation of the Saga of the Volsungs.

The mistakes and infelicities in this book are, naturally, attributable to me alone.

Jackson Crawford
Atlantic City, Wyoming
June 2, 2017

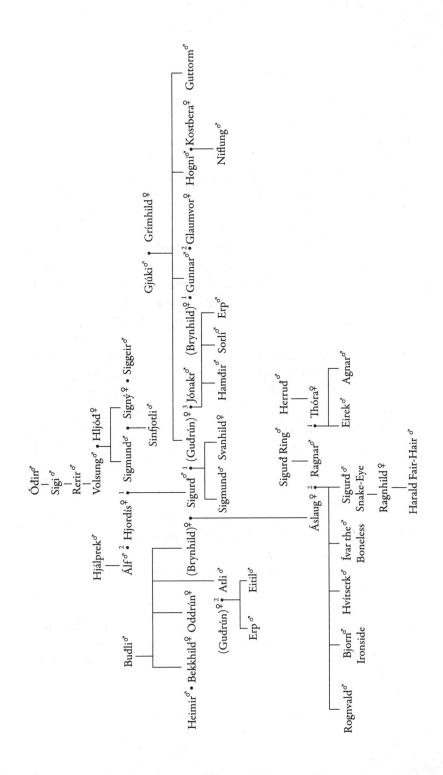

Introduction

In a Nutshell

The ill-fated romances, tragic murders, and larger-than-life wars of the Volsung family are alluded to and celebrated in numerous poems, sagas, and works of art produced in Scandinavia in the Middle Ages, and the *Saga of the Volsungs* is the most cohesive form of their story that has survived to be read in the modern age. In it, we read of Sigurd the dragon-slayer, Brynhild the Valkyrie, and the iron courage of the brothers Gunnar and Hogni and their avenging sister Gudrún.

The Saga of the Volsungs was first written in Iceland around AD 1250 by an author who had a strong familiarity with the traditional Scandinavian legends about these heroes, but the earliest manuscript in which a copy of the saga survives was not written until ca. AD 1400. In that manuscript (NKS 1824 b 4to), the Saga of the Volsungs is followed directly by a "sequel," the *Saga of Ragnar Lodbrók*, which concerns a legendary Viking chieftain of Denmark. This saga was written by a different author than the Saga of the Volsungs, and perhaps up to fifty years later, but whoever copied these two sagas together in this manuscript must have felt that they jointly formed a cohesive epic of one heroic family.

Cast of Characters, Family Tree, and Synopsis

Reading from the beginning of the Saga of the Volsungs to the end of the Saga of Ragnar Lodbrók, the two sagas tell the tale of seven generations of one family, beginning with Sigi and ending with the sons of Ragnar, although the earliest two generations are passed over quickly in the first two chapters of the Saga of the Volsungs.

There are numerous named characters in each saga, and the relationships among them are sometimes complex. The accompanying family tree shows the relationships between the principal named characters in the family of the Volsungs and their kin, who include most of the important characters in both sagas. Note that Brynhild and Guðrún both appear twice in the family tree, because of the multiple ways they are connected to other characters. Each occurrence of their names is parenthesized as a reminder.

It is important to note that *Volsung* is both the name of a single individual (the son of Rerir, and father of Sigmund and Signý) and of his family; Sigmund is thus considered "a Volsung" in addition to being the son of the man named Volsung. Inherited last names were unknown in medieval Scandinavia, but in the case of royal and otherwise outstanding families, a designation such as "the Volsungs" both honors a glorified ancestor and serves as a cohesive way of designating the family as a whole.[1]

What seem to be last names are in reality usually nicknames. For instance, while Ragnar Loðbrók is well known by that name, *Loðbrók* is not his last name but rather a nickname (literally, "shaggy pants" or "shaggy chaps"). Patronyms (names ending in *-son*) are also sometimes used, but they indicate that the person in question is in fact the son of the man named, so Sigmund Volsungsson is the son of Volsung, while Sigmund's own son Sigurð is Sigurð Sigmundsson.

The Norse god Óðin precipitates the action of the Saga of the Volsungs. Óðin is a much more complex, anxious, and deadly personality than his portrayal in popular media would usually suggest. Óðin's great purpose is his struggle to prevent or forestall his own death at Ragnarok, the foretold end of the world when the giants and monsters will kill the gods in a final battle. To this end, Óðin sends his Valkyries, mortal women granted the ability of flight, to choose the best dead

---

1. Old Norse names ending in *-ung* are typically designations for families and not for individuals, so it is likely that the original name of the individual Volsung was *Volsi*, and that his name was extended later to match the name of the family named for him; compare the name *Gjúkung* for members of the family of King *Gjúki*. This is supported by the fact that his son Sig(e)mund is called a *Wælsing* (= Old Norse *Volsung*) in Beowulf, as well as simply "son of *Wæls*," an Old English cognate of Old Norse *Volsi*. The name *Volsi* occurs in one place in Old Norse literature, in a story about the Norwegian king Ólaf Tryggvason in the manuscript *Flateyjarbók*. There, the name is applied to a stallion's preserved phallus that is worshiped by a pagan family. "Phallus," perhaps specifically "stallion's phallus," may well be the name's original meaning (the same root is found in other words for cylindrical objects), and the name of Volsung and his family might then have evoked the virility of a stallion.

warriors from earthly battlefields and convey them to his hall, Valhalla, where the warriors fight one another all day in practice for Ragnarok. Only those who die in battle have the honor of entering Valhalla; men who die by other means (and apparently all women) go to Hel, a shadowy underworld ruled by the goddess of the same name.

Óðin often travels among human beings in disguise, usually appearing as an old man who may or may not be explicitly described as lacking one eye (Óðin is missing an eye, which he gave up as the price of a drink from the mythical well of wisdom). In such disguises, he often gives a false name that suggests something about his powers, appearance, or disposition, such as *Hárbarð* ("Graybeard") or *Bolverk* ("Evil-Doer"). Since Óðin is interested in "harvesting" accomplished warriors for his army in Valhalla, he typically appears among humans in order to help a champion accomplish great heroic deeds and later to ensure his death in battle at a young age before his declining years have robbed him of his strength. Óðin is particularly attentive to the Volsungs Sigmund, Sinfjotli, and Sigurð in the first half of the Saga of the Volsungs, but then he is not seen for a long series of chapters between the death of Sigurð and the death of Sigurð's daughter Svanhild at the very end of the saga. He does not appear as a character in the Saga of Ragnar Loðbrók but is nevertheless mentioned there in a few poems that pertain to his realm of war.

Volsung is the first major human character of the Saga of the Volsungs, a king in the mythical realm of Hunland, where he builds a hall around the great tree Barnstokk (the name of the tree can be literally read as "child tree" or, more idiomatically, "family tree"). During the wedding of Volsung's daughter Signý to Siggeir, Óðin appears in disguise and lodges a sword in Barnstokk, which only Volsung's son Sigmund is able to retrieve. Siggeir later ambushes and kills his father-in-law Volsung and most of Volsung's sons. Only Sigmund escapes to live in the forest for years, plotting his vengeance. Signý disguises herself and conceives a son with Sigmund, Sinfjotli, who becomes Sigmund's apprentice and companion.

After Sigmund and Sinfjotli kill Siggeir and return to claim the throne of Hunland, Sigmund marries Borghild, who kills Sinfjotli with a poisoned drink. Sigmund remarries to Hjordís, but he dies shortly afterwards. Hjordís then gives birth to their son Sigurð. As a grown man, Sigurd later becomes famous for killing the dragon Fáfnir. After being advised by some wagtails,[2] he then meets the Valkyrie Brynhild, who has sworn an oath to marry only the man who knows no fear. Sigurd passes her test of courage by riding through a ring of fire, and the two of them promise to marry, but Sigurd leaves her side for the realm of King Gjúki, where Sigurd is magically tricked into forgetting Brynhild and then marrying Gjúki's daughter Gudrún. Disguised as Gudrún's brother Gunnar, Sigurd later rides through the ring of fire a second time and wins Brynhild's promise to marry Gunnar. Brynhild soon discovers that she has been deceived into breaking her oath, and orders Gunnar to kill Sigurd. Gunnar is unwilling to break his own oath of blood-brotherhood with Sigurd but gets his younger brother Guttorm to commit the murder. Brynhild kills herself at Sigurd's funeral and joins him in Hel.

Gudrún is married a second time to Atli, who covets Sigurd's treasure that is now owned by Gudrún's brothers Gunnar and Hogni. Atli invites them to a feast, where he ambushes and kills them. Gudrún avenges them by killing Atli and her children with him. She then attempts to drown herself and Svanhild (her daughter with Sigurd), but the waves take her instead to Jónakr, who becomes the father of her sons Hamdir, Sorli, and Erp. After Jormunrekk, a neighboring king who had intended to marry Svanhild, kills her instead for her infidelity, Gudrún's sons go to avenge their half sister, but Hamdir and Sorli kill Erp along the way, and without his help they are killed by Jormunrekk's men.

The Saga of Ragnar Lodbrók begins with Sigurd and Brynhild's daughter Áslaug, who is taken by Brynhild's brother-in-law Heimir to Norway for her own protection after the death of Brynhild. Heimir is killed by two peasants who take Áslaug in as their own daughter, renaming her Kráka ("Crow").

Meanwhile, Ragnar is a young prince of the Danes who slays a dragon and wins his first wife Thóra. Following her death, he meets Áslaug/Kráka and marries her, and they have sons named Bjorn Ironside, Hvítserk,

---

2. The white wagtail (*Motacilla alba*) is a black-and-white European bird about the size of a mockingbird. My identification of the birds that talk to Sigurd as wagtails is based on my identification of the word *igda* in the Old Norse text with the name *egde*, which is recorded for this bird in the traditional dialect of the Salten district in Norway.

Rognvald, and Ívar the Boneless (who is cursed to be without bones because his father slept with his mother too early, against her warning). Eventually Ragnar's men persuade him to leave Kráka because of her peasant origins, and Ragnar arranges to marry the daughter of a Swedish king instead. Kráka finds out about Ragnar's plan and reveals to him that she is the daughter of Sigurd and Brynhild, and as proof she prophesizes that their next son will have a snake in his eye. When she gives birth to this son, he does have an eye with this strange feature, and he is accordingly named Sigurd Snake-Eye. Realizing that his wife is in fact far nobler in origin than the Swedish princess, Ragnar breaks off the engagement, and Eirek and Agnar, his sons by his first wife, lead an invasion of Sweden in which they are killed. Áslaug changes her name once more, becoming Randalín, and joins her sons in a vengeful attack on the Swedes. Afterwards the surviving sons of Ragnar (collectively designated the Ragnarssons) engage in a number of celebrated Viking raids, and Ragnar himself is finally killed in a pit of snakes after he attempts to fulfill a boastful oath to conquer England with only two ships. His sons travel to England and avenge their father by conquering a large part of it and torturing Ella, the English king responsible for putting him to death.

The Making of the Sagas

Saga is a word borrowed directly into English in modern times from Icelandic. In Icelandic the word can mean simply "history" or "story," but in English it is used especially to refer to the long, novel-like stories written in Iceland during the 1200s and 1300s AD. During these centuries, the Icelanders were not only busy writing the relatively realistic sagas of their own adventurous ancestors but also were seeking to preserve the myths of the gods and legendary heroes who once had been venerated throughout Scandinavia. It was during this century that the Poetic Edda was compiled, containing several poems that are still our most important source for Scandinavia's pre-Christian mythology. Among those poems are many that deal not with the gods but with the Volsung family, especially the dragon-slayer Sigurd.

The author of the Saga of the Volsungs knew many of these poems and quotes them often in the saga. Quoting from these old poems, some of which date back to the Viking Age, which was already long in the past when this saga was written, might have helped establish an air of authenticity and tradition for the saga's original audience. But the author of the saga does not simply retell the story of these poems in prose. Each poem in the Poetic Edda focuses on one or a few specific incidents, and many of the poems tell contradictory narratives, since they were composed at different times in far-flung places by poets who knew (and helped shape) variant forms of the stories. The saga, however, unites material from many different poems in the Poetic Edda, together with other sources, into one reasonably streamlined story.

While the saga author does a remarkably good job of rendering a readable, cohesive story out of these many conflicting traditions, the seams are still visible in places in the saga. For instance, in the poem *Sigrdrífumál* (*Sigrdrifumal*)[3] preserved in the Poetic Edda, the hero Sigurd encounters a Valkyrie named Sigrdrífa who gives him advice after he awakens her from her enchanted slumber inside a ring of fire. Much of this poem is quoted and paraphrased in chapters 20–21 of the Saga of the Volsungs, but here the words of Sigrdrífa are attributed to Brynhild. It is unclear in the Poetic Edda whether Sigrdrífa and Brynhild are the same person, but the saga author unambiguously presents them as one, never mentioning the name Sigrdrífa.

After this first encounter with Brynhild, the saga has Sigurd ride away to the home of Brynhild's foster-father Heimir, where he finds Brynhild again, living much as any other woman might. It is never explained how or why Brynhild has suddenly moved, and she and Sigurd hardly seem to know each other at all when they meet again in chapter 24. Moreover, in chapter 27, when Sigurd rides through Brynhild's ring of fire a second time, the text explicitly says that no one has done it before, and in chapters 29 and 31 we read hints of another tradition in which Gunnar had to threaten her foster-father Budli for her hand in marriage. It could be that some of the confusion arises from the mixing of traditions about the meeting and courting of two different Valkyries, one who was possibly originally named Sigrdrífa and the other Brynhild. Or perhaps Sigrdrífa (which means roughly "victory-driver") was not originally a

---

3. Throughout this book, the titles of poems in the Poetic Edda are given first in the Old Norse spelling used in this book (see *Language and Pronunciation*, later in the Introduction), followed in parentheses by the more anglicized titles in *The Poetic Edda: Stories of the Norse Gods and Heroes* (Hackett, 2015).

separate woman's name but rather a poetic title for the Valkyrie's role as chooser of victors and losers on the battlefield, and in some branches of the tradition this became misunderstood as a name. Nevertheless, the way the saga author handles the multiple meetings with Brynhild shows a desire to incorporate as much traditional material as possible, while attempting to forge it all into a straightforward chronology of events.[4]

The Saga of Ragnar Loðbrók also frequently quotes short and long poems, but these are from a different school of Norse poetry. While the poems in the Poetic Edda are relatively simple in style, the Norse kings and noblemen of the Viking Age (and the first centuries afterwards) favored an extraordinarily complex style of poetry known in English as *skaldic*, from Old Norse *skáld*, "poet." Skaldic poems are typically eight-line stanzas, with rigid rules about what syllables in a line must alliterate and rhyme with what other syllables. In order to adhere to these rules, skaldic poets were required to create *kennings*, compact metaphors that require deciphering, such as "wound-reed" for "arrow" or "blood-swan" for "raven." Such kennings, in rephrasing the intended referent in new, cryptic words, allowed the skaldic poet ample room to demonstrate his creativity while enabling him to find words that alliterated or rhymed in the correct places when more conventional wording might have not.[5]

The debt that both sagas owe to older poetry is a reminder that the saga authors, not unlike scholars and readers in the twenty-first century,

---

4. There were numerous traditional variants of many other parts of the story too, and in some cases the mixing of these variants has occurred already in the poems of the Poetic Edda that the author of the Saga of the Volsungs relies on. For example, while the author of the saga has chosen to relate only one version of the story of Sigurd's murder (the one in which Sigurd is murdered by Guttorm while in bed), Brynhild's dying speech in chapter 31 refers to "the men who were killed with Sigurd," which looks like the imperfectly concealed fragment of a very different story. The saga's author, however, is simply following the poem *Sigurðarkviða en skamma (Sigurtharkvitha en skamma)* here (which is the source of much of the saga's account of Sigurd's murder and funeral), in which Brynhild makes the same confusing remark.

5. Because kennings are artifacts of the Norse poet's art and require an audience that understands the original language and its poetic demands, I have done the task of "unpacking" or fully translating them in my translations of skaldic poems in the Saga of Ragnar Loðbrók, as I had already done in my published translations of the poems of the Poetic Edda that are quoted in the Saga of the Volsungs. This allows the reader to appreciate the context and meaning of a poem fully, rather than be forced to assemble its meaning line-by-line from glosses in footnotes or parentheses.

were already fairly late in the chain of transmission—they were receiving, and then working within, what was already a centuries-old tradition concerning the heroes they wrote about. And they were removed not just in time but also in place from the origin of these stories. While the two sagas in this volume were written down in Iceland and have a prominent place in the legacy of Icelandic literature, the stories considerably predate the settlement of that country, and no part of their action takes place in Iceland.

Iceland was settled by Norwegians and Norwegian colonists from the British Isles beginning during the Viking Age in the AD 870s, and the first generation of settlers brought with them a wealth of tales about gods and heroes from their homes in Scandinavia. Ragnar Loðbrók and his sons were famous throughout the Viking world, and the heroes of the Volsung clan were famous throughout Scandinavia and beyond, in all the other countries where Germanic languages were spoken in the Middle Ages, including England and Germany.

The distant origins of many of the scenes and characters of the Saga of the Volsungs are traceable to historical events and people in the centuries of the decline and end of the Roman Empire (ca. AD 300–500), when members of different Germanic tribes at times joined Roman forces as the Empire's defenders and at times destroyed, ransacked, and plundered its borders and cities. In the same period, the Huns, a nomadic people of the Asian steppes, swept into Europe from the east and waged war on the Roman Empire. Other Germanic war bands allied themselves with the invading Hunnish forces, and in fact it is the Gothic nickname *Attila* (literally "little daddy"; *Atli* in Old Norse) for the great Hunnish leader that has survived to become famous today, rather than his unknown native Hunnish name. Attila, who died in AD 451 or 453, is incorporated into the legends of the Volsung family not as the leader of bands of nomadic Hunnish warriors but as the king of a stable realm and, in the main Norse tradition at least, as the brother of Brynhild.

Similarly, Gjúki and his son Gunnar appear to reflect a historical Gibica and Gundaharius, who are named as kings of the Burgundians in what is now eastern France and western Switzerland; Gundaharius was killed in a battle with Huns in AD 437. The Old Norse name *Jormunrekk* would be **Airmanareiks* (i.e., **Ermanariks*) in Gothic, and in fact history mentions an *Ermanaricus* who was king of the East Goths living near the Black Sea who died in AD 375. Writing in the AD 500s, the Gothic historian Jordanes says that two brothers, *Sarus* and *Ammius* (= Old Norse *Sorli* and *Hamdir*), killed Ermanaricus to avenge the murder of their sister *Sunilda* (= Old Norse *Svanhild*), a story not at all dissimilar to the last chapters of the Saga of the Volsungs. The Old English form of the name is *Eormanric,* and a king of this name is briefly alluded to in the Old English poem *Deor,* showing that some version of this story must also have been told in early medieval England.

Some have seen the distant origin of Brynhild and Sigurd in the early medieval Frankish queen named Brunhilda and her first husband, King Sigebert I of Austrasia (an early Germanic kingdom in northeastern France and west-central Germany). Sigebert was murdered around AD 575 in the course of a long war against his half brother, but he was survived for many decades by Brunhilda, who led a long life in and out of royal power, marked by numerous violent acts of vengeance, and was finally killed by being torn apart by wild horses, according to the *Liber historiae Francorum* (Book of the History of the Franks, AD 700s). While Brunhilda's name is cognate with Old Norse *Brynhild,* and her life was very dramatic, there are not many convincing parallels between her story and Brynhild's, nor between Sigebert's and Sigurd's. The name *Sigebert* shares a first element (*Sig(e)-*, "victory") with *Sigurd,* but the second elements are unrelated; Old Norse *Sigurd* (earlier *Sigvard*) means "victory-guardian."

Casting even deeper into history, an old hypothesis connects Sigurd with the Germanic leader who defeated three Roman legions in the Battle of the Teutoburger Wald in AD 9. This warrior's name is remembered in Roman sources as *Arminius,* which may be a Latinization of the Proto-Germanic word **harjamannaz,* which would simply mean "soldier" and might have been a title rather than the man's name. Since many of Arminius' family members are recorded with names that begin with *Sig-*, it has been posited that his true name was something similar to *Sigurd,* and that the great historical warrior's triumph over an overwhelming military force became the legendary hero's triumph over a dragon. The presence of an area called *Knetterheide* (resembling the place called *Gnitaheid* where Sigurd kills Fáfnir) in the vicinity of the battle site helped fuel this notion, which became popular in the nineteenth century. But this is a great deal of speculation to base on the imperfectly recorded names of Arminius' relatives in Roman histories, and few modern scholars accept the Arminius connection.

Ragnar may be distantly rooted in the memory of a real Viking of that name who raided deep into present-day France in AD 845, although both the *Annales Xantenses* (Chronicles of Xanten) and the *Miracula Sancti Germani* (Miracles of St. Germanus), which are nearly contemporary accounts, say that this Viking leader died of sickness later the same year. If the Icelandic scholar Snorri Sturluson (AD 1179–1241) is to be believed, Bragi Boddason, regarded by legend as the founder of skaldic poetry, was a contemporary of Ragnar and composed his famous poem *Ragnarsdrápa* for the man himself. However, the Ragnar of the saga has clearly become a figure of legend and a near-contemporary of the much more ancient Volsungs, and it is doubtful that these legends preserve any real memory of his accomplishments. It is also possible that the name or nickname *Loðbrók* originally belonged to a different person entirely than the historical Ragnar, as the two names are not mentioned together as one man, Ragnar Loðbrók, earlier than in the work of Icelandic historian Ari Thorgilsson (AD 1067–1148).

Historical sources mention some individuals who may correspond with Ragnar's sons, but their names and relations are not easily reconciled with what the saga tells of them. In the Latin *Gesta Normannorum Ducum* (History of the Dukes of Normandy, ca. AD 1070), the Norman historian Guillaume de Jumièges mentions a Bjorn Ironside who was the son of a King Loðbrók, and at least two medieval French chronicles mention a Viking raider named *Berno* (= Old Norse *Bjorn*, Proto-Norse **Bernuz*) in the 850s AD who might be the same man. Numerous sources from inside and outside Scandinavia name sons such as Ubbi and "Anstignus" (= Old Norse *Hástein*?), names that do not occur in the saga at all.

The Anglo-Saxon Chronicle tells of a "Great Heathen Army" that raided in eastern England in AD 865 and killed a Northumbrian king named Ælla in AD 867; among the leaders of this army, the Old English historian Æthelweard mentions an I(g)uuar, whose name corresponds to an early Danish form of *Ívar*. Later English sources elaborate on this story considerably but probably not with any historical basis. Irish annals also mention an *Imhar* (pronounced like *Ívar*) as king over the Norsemen in Ireland and Britain, who died in AD 873; he is probably the same man. Many scholars have seen this I(g)uuar/Imhar as the basis of the Ívar the Boneless of the saga, but there is no historical reason to think he was the son of Ragnar (the name of Imhar's father is given in Irish annals as *Gofraid*), nor to assume that the saga records more than a greatly embellished account of his record as a war leader in the British Isles.

Looking forward into history from the end of the Saga of Ragnar Loðbrók, in chapter 18 Ragnar's son Sigurð Snake-Eye is credited as the grandfather of Harald Fairhair, the first king of the united kingdom of Norway and founder of the medieval Norwegian royal dynasty, who died ca. AD 930. By connecting the Norwegian royal family with this preeminent family of Norse heroes, the Saga of Ragnar Loðbrók was part of a tradition that glorified living rulers and helped justify their claims to power in a time when history and legend were even more easily conflated than they are today.

Whatever their possible historical origins, these heroes were completely the province of legend by the time the Saga of the Volsungs was composed in Iceland in the 1200s. But it was not only in Iceland that forms of their stories were being told.

The Danish historian Saxo Grammaticus, in book 8 of his Latin *Gesta Danorum* (History of the Danes) from around AD 1200, relates a nearly identical story to that at the end of the Saga of the Volsungs about *Jarmericus* (= Old Norse *Jormunrekk*), and how he killed his bride *Swanilde* (= Old Norse *Svanhild*) at the instigation of his evil counselor *Bicco* (= Old Norse *Bikki*), who told him that Swanilde had slept with his son. Swanilde is avenged by unnamed kinsmen, and, just as in the Saga of the Volsungs, Jarmericus is killed by having his arms and legs chopped off before the god Óðin tells his men how to kill his attackers. Saxo mentions a *Guthrune* (= Old Norse *Guðrún*) as well, but only as a witch who assists Swanilde's avengers.

In book 9 of *Gesta Danorum*, Saxo also tells his own version of the story of *Regnerus* (= Old Norse *Ragnar*) and his sons, which in some ways is strikingly similar to the Norse saga printed in this volume, even down to Ragnar's last words as he dies in the snake-pit. However, other details are remarkably different. For instance, according to Saxo, Sigurð Snake-Eye received his namesake feature because the god Óðin sprinkled a magic dust into his eyes after he was wounded in battle. Saxo also makes Thóra the mother of Sigurð and Ivar, and gives Ragnar more wives, including a warrior woman named *Lagertha* (= Old Norse *Hladgerd*), who is not mentioned in the Old Norse saga at all. No equivalent of Áslaug, who is Ragnar's second wife in the saga and his connection to the Volsung legend, is mentioned by Saxo, though Saxo's book 5 mentions a certain Craca (who is incidentally married to an unrelated Regnerus) who gives magical aid to her stepson Ericus. It is difficult to think that this legend is not connected in some way to the story that became Áslaug's, as she is named *Kráka* when Ragnar meets her in the saga, and she later shows great concern for avenging her stepson Eirek.

South of Scandinavia, the epic poem called the *Nibelungenlied* was written, probably in Austria, in Middle High German around AD 1200. The Nibelungenlied is perhaps the best-known version of the Volsung legend today, and it shares many details in common with the parts of the Saga of the Volsungs that it overlaps with (roughly, chapters 26–38). The Nibelungenlied centers on the dragon-slaying hero Sivrit, whose name (often rendered as *Siegfried*) shares a first but not a second element related to the name *Sigurd*. He is renowned for slaying a dragon and for seizing a great treasure, but these are separate events in his life in the Nibelungenlied, and they are told of only at second-hand. Sivrit wishes to marry the sister of *Gunther* (= Old Norse *Gunnar*), who is named *Kriemhilt* (the name is related to Old Norse *Grímhild*, but the character is equivalent to Gudrún). In order to do so, he helps Gunther win the hand of *Prünhilt* (= Old Norse *Brynhild*), who will only marry a man who can defeat her in three tests of strength and skill. Sivrit uses his magical cloak of invisibility to help Gunther win. Later, Sivrit must also invisibly subdue the supernaturally strong Prünhilt for Gunther on their wedding night, and in the process he takes a distinctive ring and a belt from her. Ten years afterwards, Kriemhilt shows these stolen items to Prünhilt during a dispute about their relative ranks and gloats that Prünhilt has been Sivrit's lover. To defend Gunther's honor, his advisor *Hagen* (= Old Norse *Hogni*) murders Sivrit during a hunting trip. Kriemhilt later marries *Etzel* (= Old Norse *Atli*) and invites Gunther and Hagen to a feast, where she has Gunther and then Hagen killed in a failed effort to learn where Hagen has hidden Sivrit's treasure in the Rhine. Kriemhilt herself is then killed by the hero Hildebrant.

Even from this brief summary of the story's events, the reader can see important differences from the Saga of the Volsungs, in spite of their broadly similar plots. The German Kriemhilt invites her brother Gunther into a trap in order to avenge her murdered husband on him, whereas it is her brothers that the Norse Guđrún avenges on her second husband after *he* treacherously invites them into an ambush. The Nibelungenlied also portrays many of the principal characters very differently, giving us, for instance, the scheming, treacherous Hagen, a half-elven advisor to Gunther, who has little in common with Gunnar's level-headed, honorable brother Hogni in the Norse tradition. There are also striking differences in the details of the narrative; Sivrit does not drink the dragon's blood but bathes in it instead, and doing so makes him impervious to weapons everywhere on his body except for a single spot where a leaf fell on him before his bath.

Moreover, the Nibelungenlied was composed in a vastly different cultural milieu, that of the courtly society of high medieval European knights. The sagas composed in Iceland at this time did not entirely escape influence from the same culture (consider the almost knightly description of Sigurd and his second encounter with Brynhild in chapters 22–24 of the Saga of the Volsungs), but Iceland was never a land of feudal barons and chivalrous knights, and these make a fanciful and foreign impression when they appear in the sagas. Beyond its similarities and differences with the Saga of the Volsungs, the Nibelungenlied is fascinating in its own right as an example of an early medieval, "barbarian" heroic epic adapted into this chivalric idiom, just as a closely related story was adapted into the saga in Iceland.

Much earlier, the Old English poem *Beowulf*, probably composed at some time between AD 800 and 1000, mentions two Volsung heroes by name, *Sigemund Waelsing* (= Old Norse *Sigmund*, the *Volsung*) and his nephew *Fitela* (corresponding to the last part of the compound Norse name Sin-*fjotli*). In fact, the story told about Sigemund in *Beowulf* portrays him, rather than his unmentioned son, as the dragon-slayer; whether this is a more "original" version of the story or simply another variant is unknown. The digression about Sigemund is in *Beowulf*, verses 1748–1801 (see the translation by Ringler under *Further Reading*, below).

Other versions of the stories told in these two sagas were preserved in Old Norse as well. Some early skaldic poems (including Bragi Boddason's *Ragnarsdrápa*) make important allusions to events in the Volsung mythos, and Snorri Sturluson's *Edda* (usually called the Prose

Edda to distinguish it from the Poetic Edda) tells a condensed version of the Sigurd legend that is similar to the Saga of the Volsungs. The Norwegian *Thidreks saga af Bern* (Saga of Thidrek of Bern) is a thirteenth-century compendium of numerous heroes and their legends, and it contains a highly divergent version of the story of Sigurd that is more closely related to the German tradition of the Nibelungenlied than it is to the later Saga of the Volsungs, which it nevertheless influenced. A short Icelandic saga (*tháttr*) called *Ragnarssona tháttr* (Story of Ragnar's Sons) survives that is roughly contemporary with the Saga of Ragnar Lodbrók and preserves a related story of his late life and some of the accomplishments of his sons, and a skaldic poem composed in the 1100s in the Hebrides called *Krákumál* is put in the mouth of Ragnar as he dies in the snake-pit. Traditional oral ballads about the Volsung heroes and Ragnar Lodbrók survived late enough in Scandinavia to be recorded in the sixteenth through twentieth centuries; several of the most notable come from the Faroe Islands (where examples include *Sjúrdar kvædi*, "Sigurd's Song"; *Brynhildar táttur*, "Brynhild's Story"; and *Ragnars kvædi*, "Ragnar's Poem"), Norway (including numerous variants of the ballad of *Sigurd Svein*, "Boy Sigurd"), and Denmark (including ballads about *Kragelil*, a character related to Áslaug/Kráka).

The heroes of the Saga of the Volsungs were remembered in more than just narrative tales and poems. Many artifacts survive that illustrate part of the legend, including runestones such as Sö 101 from Ramsund, Sweden, known as the Ramsund Carving, carved probably between AD 1000 and 1050. The Ramsund Carving depicts several incidents from Sigurd's slaying of the dragon Fáfnir, including small details such as the burning of his finger on the roasting dragon's heart. Such a close correspondence in small details with the story related in the Saga of the Volsungs shows that parts of the Sigurd narrative had already achieved something very like the form they have in the surviving saga when this stone was carved two hundred years earlier. Various other Viking Age runestones and picture stones from Sweden depict parts of the Volsung legend; Gunnar's death in the snake-pit was a particularly popular motif. In Norway, the doors of the Hylestad Stave Church (built ca. AD 1200) are carved with scenes from the life of Sigurd and his slaying of Fáfnir, as well as Gunnar's death in the snake-pit. And in England, some have interpreted the carvings on the very early Franks Casket (probably AD 700s) as containing scenes from the Volsung story, including the mourning of Gudrún and Grani over the grave of Sigurd.

Indirectly, the same stories and their heroes continue to be famous today. The Saga of the Volsungs strongly influenced Richard Wagner's *Ring* cycle and J. R. R. Tolkien's fantasy novels, and through them numerous other works. Motifs and scenes borrowed from the Saga of the Volsungs appear throughout Tolkien's work, such as in the broken sword reforged for Aragorn in *The Lord of the Rings* and the slaying of the dragon by Túrin Turambar in *The Silmarillion*. Tolkien also dealt directly with the Norse source material in *The Legend of Sigurd and Gudrún*, his creative attempt to reconstruct an incomplete poem of the Poetic Edda that contributed much to the surviving Saga of the Volsungs. Meanwhile, it is not too much to say that Wagner's *Der Ring des Nibelungen* is a reimagining of the Saga of the Volsungs, although with numerous elements adapted from the German tradition of the Nibelungenlied, together with many elements that are Wagner's own imagination (such as the power to rule the world that is granted by the ring, which does not resemble the simple cursed ring of the saga). Ragnar Lodbrók has also gained new fame in the twentieth and twenty-first centuries. He is the chief protagonist in a blockbuster film (*The Vikings* [1958], starring Kirk Douglas) and in the enormously popular television series *Vikings* that began airing in 2013. His story has also inspired novels, including science fiction writer Harry Harrison's *The Hammer and the Cross* (1993), which incorporates a great deal of material from the Saga of Ragnar Lodbrók.

Seen in a wider context that takes in both their ancient roots and the widespread and long-lasting fame of their heroes, these two sagas stand out not as the sources of a mythical tradition but as the culmination of it. The Saga of the Volsungs, in particular, is the masterpiece of an author who inherited a magnificent and deep-rooted set of conflicting but related traditions, and made from them a sweeping story that has become one of the longest-enduring and most influential sagas.

Culture and Values

The Saga of the Volsungs and the Saga of Ragnar Lodbrók were composed in Iceland centuries after that island-republic had been converted to Christianity, an event traditionally dated to the year AD 1000. Yet Christian Iceland was isolated by its distance from the rest of Scandinavia and Europe, and maintained independent practices in culture and literature, many of which remained more similar to those of the Viking Age than to those of contemporary societies in late medieval Europe. The culture and values presented in the sagas are grounded in those of this older, pre-Christian layer of Icelandic society, while not being impervious to the influence of later medieval Christian thought.

The Viking-like society presented in these sagas is warlike and tribal, with social mores and expectations based on the family, not the individual, as the unit of value. With the availability of natural resources sharply limited in Viking Age Scandinavia by its harsh climate and sparse farmland, neighboring families and small states often existed in a state of violent competition for survival. Naked aggression was not necessarily considered wrong if it advanced one's wealth and reputation and that of one's family. Readers will note that, in chapter 8 of the Saga of the Volsungs, when the hero Sigmund determines that the young Sinfjotli is still too inexperienced to help him avenge his father, he takes Sinfjotli into the woods to train him by killing and robbing travelers for their valuables. This in no way diminishes their moral stature in their society, as their victims are unrelated to them. It would be the responsibility of their victims' families to take vengeance for them, but for Sigmund and Sinfjotli, supremely capable warriors of the Volsung clan, the threat of vengeance from the kinsmen of incidental victims must have seemed of little practical concern, and virtually no ethical concern.

The promise of mutual revenge bound a family together in a feuding world, and thus there was a special horror for the notion of accidentally or knowingly doing damage to one's own relatives. Nonetheless, the heroes of the sagas are sometimes forced to take action against their own families, usually because of the ironclad force of their sworn words and boasts. The sagas depict a world in which a person's words are absolutely binding, no matter the consequences—which are often tragic. The greatest tragedy of the Saga of the Volsungs is the murder of Sigurd, which is brought about because Brynhild has been tricked into breaking her vow that she will marry only a man who knows no fear. Since not Brynhild but Gudrún is married to the fearless Sigurd, Brynhild insists that her husband Gunnar must kill him. But even here, Gunnar and his brother Hogni will not break their oaths of blood-brotherhood with

Sigurd, and Gunnar instead must get his brother Guttorm, who was too young to swear an oath to Sigurd, to commit the murder.

Norse society also had rigid expectations of different social classes, which are reflected in nearly every chapter of these two sagas, beginning in chapter 1 of the Saga of the Volsungs when Sigi, progenitor of the Volsung family, is made an outlaw for killing Bredi, another man's slave, out of jealousy at his superior hunting skills. In chapter 12, Queen Hjordís exchanges clothes with her unnamed servant while they are in hiding, and orders the servant to pretend to be her. But Álf, who finds them, is suspicious that something is wrong, since the "servant" is more courtly and attractive than the woman he thinks is the queen, and his suspicions are soon confirmed.

An even starker example of these attitudes is in chapter 9 of the Saga of Ragnar Lodbrók. The Danish Viking and ruler Ragnar has married a beautiful woman he believes to be named Kráka (Crow), who he also believes is the daughter of two poor and ugly peasants. In spite of Kráka's fantastic beauty, however, Ragnar's men later pressure him to take a wife from a better family, and so he arranges to marry Ingibjorg, the daughter of a Swedish king. When he comes home from making the engagement, his wife has heard the news, and she pleads with him not to abandon her, because she in fact can claim even nobler birth than Ingibjorg. Kráka now confesses to Ragnar that her true name is Áslaug, and that she is the daughter of the great hero Sigurd and the Valkyrie Brynhild. As proof, she says she will soon give birth to a son who will have a snake in his eye. When the child is born, Ragnar sees the proof in his eye and remains with the wife who, after all, was noble enough to be married to him. Such considerations may seem hardly romantic to readers today, but the anxiety of a family losing face by being tied to people of lower rank was no trivial fear in the struggle for survival and prestige between competing clans.

While the domains of war and local government were largely the province of men in Viking times, one of the most striking characteristics of the two sagas in this volume is the prominent role played by women characters, especially Signý, Brynhild, and Gudrún in the Saga of the Volsungs, and Áslaug in the Saga of Ragnar Lodbrók. Far from the passive, one-dimensional princesses of so much medieval or fantasy literature, these are forceful, bold women who are steadfast in their purpose (in fact, Brynhild's unwavering commitment to her oaths is at the core of the saga's tragedy) and who even physically fight alongside men (as when Guđrún takes up weapons to help her brothers in battle in chapter 36 of the Saga of the Volsungs, or when Áslaug joins the army of her sons in chapter 11 of the Saga of Ragnar Lođbrók).

It is usually women in these sagas who are capable of peering into the future and interpreting dreams and other signs. Brynhild, for instance, is shown to have this power in chapter 25 of the Saga of the Volsungs when she correctly interprets Guđrún's dream, foretelling the conflict the two women will have over Sigurd. Similarly, in chapters 34 and 35, Hogni and Gunnar's wives try to dissuade them from making a journey based on clear signs they have seen in dreams and written in runes (and the men's interpretations of their dreams are wildly wrong, though this seems to be a product of their stubbornness rather than ignorance). However, the revealing of the future in prophecies or dreams is never effective in the sagas; what modern readers might regard as "spoilers" were evidently seen differently by a medieval audience. Even after a very direct and specific warning about the future, the characters in the sagas typically behave as if they had no forewarning whatsoever—or, perhaps, they consider it more important to face a bad fate well than to try to fight the inevitable.

Despite their preeminent roles as instigators, participants, and fore-seers of the sagas' action, the women of these sagas often are forced to act as subordinates to their male relations, especially in matters of marriage—as Signý is forced by her father, Volsung, to marry Siggeir against her will, and Guđrún, while she loves Sigurd, is offered to him in marriage essentially as a prize for his military support of her father and brothers. In chapter 27 of the the Saga of the Volsungs, Gunnar rides to the home of Brynhild's father Buđli to propose his marriage to her before she has ever heard of him. Yet the sagas also seem to acknowl-edge men's wrongdoing when they ignore women's wishes, as neither Signý's nor Brynhild's forced marriages are happy, and both marriages lead to terrible consequences for both families involved.

Language and Pronunciation

The two sagas in this volume were composed in Old Norse, the written language of medieval Iceland and Norway. This language, sometimes called Old West Norse, is the direct ancestor of today's Icelandic, Norwegian, and

Faroese languages, and is very closely related to Old East Norse, the ancestor of Danish and Swedish. Old Norse is also a "first cousin" to other old Germanic languages, such as Gothic, Old English, and Old High German, and thus distantly related (as an "aunt" or "uncle") to modern Germanic languages such as English, German, and Dutch.

Old Norse was written using the Roman alphabet (the alphabet used for English and most other Western European languages today) beginning in approximately AD 1150, with the addition of some new letters for sounds that the Roman alphabet was not designed to accommodate. In the interest of readability, modern editors and translators of Norse literature must make decisions on how to render these letters, and invariably these decisions must sometimes contradict one another's. The issue is complicated by several considerations, including the fact that many of these special Norse/Icelandic letters resemble more familiar letters that represent completely different sounds, as well as the variation in spelling in medieval manuscripts.

In this volume, I have rendered Old Norse personal names in a less anglicized form than in my translation of the Poetic Edda.[6] The names of humans and gods are written essentially as they are in standard, "textbook" Old Norse, with the following modifications and considerations:

1. The letter *þ* (þorn) is rendered as *th* (thus *Þóra* becomes *Thóra*). The letter *þ* represents the sound of *th* in English *worth* or *breath*, but the letter is frequently mistaken for *p*.

2. The letter *ð* (eð), which in origin is a rounded medieval letter *d* with a crossbar, is rendered as a straight-backed, modern *d* with a crossbar, *đ* (thus *Guđrún*). This letter represents the sound of *th* in English *worthy* or *breathe*. The less common straight-backed version of this letter is used because the rounded version is frequently mistaken for *o*.

---

6. In that volume, only the twenty-six letters used in English are employed, so the length of vowels is ignored, and both *þ* and *ð* are printed as *th*. In the present book, when the titles of the poems of the Poetic Edda are referenced, they are printed first according to this volume's rules for anglicizing names and then in parentheses by the form their titles have in that book, e.g., *Hamđismál (Hamthismal)*.

3. The letter ǫ (o caudata) is rendered as *o* (thus *Hǫgni* is rendered as *Hogni*). In Old Norse, the letter ǫ represented the sound of *o* in English *or*. This vowel has become *ö* in Modern Icelandic and *o* in Modern Norwegian. Some editors and translators use Modern Icelandic *ö* here, but this encourages an anachronistic pronunciation. Unfortunately there are few fonts or digital readers that successfully render ǫ, and the letter is easily mistaken for *q*, but the use of plain *o* to render this vowel is not unknown from Old Norse manuscripts. The most important names with this vowel are *Volsung*, *Sinfjotli*, *Hjordis*, *Hogni*, *Jormunrekk*, and *Sorli*.

4. In accordance with the usual convention of modern translators, the -*r* that ends many names in the subject (nominative) case is removed. Old Norse is a highly inflected language, and certain endings are added to the root of a word when it performs different functions—for example, *Sigmundr* is the man's name when he is the subject of a verb ("*Sigmundr* hit me"), but his name is *Sigmund* without the -*r* when he is the object ("I hit *Sigmund*"). This grammatical ending appears as a second -*r* or -*n* on masculine names that end in in -*r* (such as *Ragnarr*, *Ívarr*) or -*n* (such as *Óðinn*), and this is removed by the same convention (*Ragnar*, *Ívar*, *Óðin*). However, the -*r* at the end of a name is left intact when it is part of the name's root and not simply a grammatical ending; the only important name of this kind in this book is *Jónakr*. By convention, the final -*r* is also left intact in names that end in -*ir*, such as *Heimir* and *Hamdir*.

5. The vowels *æ* and *ø* (*œ*) are kept separate, as they are in the oldest Icelandic texts and in Old Norwegian (thus *Hønir* rather than *Hænir*).

I have followed the same guidelines in rendering Old Norse place-names, but I have substituted modern place-names when these are available in order to facilitate comparison with good modern maps (thus Swedish *Götaland* and *Uppsala*, and Danish *Fyn* and *Samsø*, rather than Old Norse *Gautland*, *Uppsalir*, *Fjón*, *Sámsey*). In dealing with common nouns, where an English rendering of the Old Norse word is already widespread and popular, I have used that instead of directly transliterating the Old Norse word according to the guidelines above: thus I write *Valhalla* and *Valkyrie* instead of the more authentic or consistent *Valhǫll* and *Valkyrja*. I have usually translated nicknames (Bjorn *Ironside*, Sigurd *Snake-Eye*), but I have left Ragnar *Loðbrók* (shaggy-pants) untranslated because Ragnar is well known under that name in the modern world.

In reading aloud the Old Norse names in the translation, a few ground rules should be kept in mind. The accent is always on the first syllable of a word, thus *SIG-urd*, not *sig-URÐ*, and *BRYN-hild*, not *bryn-HILD*, and so on. The pronunciation of Old Norse in the AD 1200s (i.e., approximately during the time when these two sagas were originally composed) can be reconstructed with great confidence using the tools of historical linguistics, and this reconstructed medieval pronunciation is easier to learn and more historically authentic than the Modern Icelandic pronunciation favored by many today. The Old Norse pronunciation of most consonants is similar enough to the Modern English pronunciation to require no comment. The most important facts to note are these:

ð is pronounced as the English *th* in *worthy* (not *worth*); thus *Sigurd* is pronounced *SIG-urth*, ending on the the *th* sound of English *breathe* (not *breath*).

f is pronounced as *v* unless at the beginning of a word; thus the name *Fáfnir* is pronounced close to *FOV-near*, and *Álf* as *OLV*.

g is pronounced as in *go*, never with the sound of *j* as in *gin*; thus the second syllable of *Regin* is like that of *begin*, not like the liquor *gin*.

h can occur in the combinations *hj* (*Hjordís*), *hl* (*Hlymdalir*), *hr* (*Hreidmar*), and *hv* (*Hvítserk*). *Hj* is pronounced with the *hy* sound of the *h* in English *Houston* or *hue*, and *hv* probably with the *hw* sound of older American English *wh* in *what* or *whale* (see also *j* and *v*, below). The sounds of *hl* and *hr* are, similarly, produced by pronouncing the *h* in English *he* followed by an *l* or *r* before the vowel.

j is pronounced as the English *y* in young, or the German *j* in *ja*; thus *Jormunrekk* is pronounced *Yorm-un-wreck*. The sequence *hj* is pronounced *hy* as the *h* in English *Houston* or *hue*.

r is a trill (as in Spanish) or a tap (as in Scots). In a name such as *Jónakr* or *Baldr*, the *-r* constitutes a separate syllable, pronounced not unlike the final syllable in American English *water* or *bitter*.

s is pronounced as in *bass*, never with the sound of *z* as in *has*; thus *Áslaug* is pronounced *OSS-loug*, not *OZ-loug*.

th (þ) is pronounced as the English *th* in *worth* or *breath* (not *worthy* or *breathe*), thus *Thór* is correctly pronounced as it is usually pronounced in English (his name is not pronounced like *tore* or *tour*, as it is in modern Scandinavian languages or German).

v is pronounced as the English *v* in *very*. It is likely that a *v* after another consonant was pronounced as *w* (a pattern not unknown in modern languages, for example in the pronunciation of the letter *w* in Afrikaans), so *Hvítabǿ* would begin with the *hw* sound of older American English "where," and *Svanhild* would be pronounced as *SWAN-hild*.

Vowels without the acute length mark (´) are pronounced as in Spanish, so *a* is the *o* of American English *got, e* is the *e* of *pet, i* is the *ee* of *feet, o* is approximately the *oa* in *boat* (pronouncing this word with a northern Wisconsin accent will be nearer the actual Scandinavian pronunciation), and *u* is the *oo* of *boot*. The vowel *y* is similar to *u*, but further forward in the mouth, like the German *ü* or the vowel in a "surfer" pronunciation of *dude* or *tune*. The letter *y* is not used as a consonant in Old Norse (see *j*, above). The vowel *æ* is pronounced as the *a* in *cash*, and the vowel *ø* has a pronunciation somewhat like the *i* in *bird* (more authentically, the German *ö* or the Norwegian *ø*). A vowel with the acute length mark (´) is pronounced with the same sound as the equivalent unmarked vowel, but the syllable lasts a few fractions of a second longer (compare the words *hat* and *had* in English, where the vowel is longer in the second word than in the first). The exception is long *á*, which is pronounced with more rounding of the lips than the short vowel, similar to the *o* in a northern New Jersey pronunciation of *coffee*.

The combination *au* is pronounced like the *ou* of *house*, while *ei* is the *ai* of *rain*. The combination *ey* is somewhat similar to the *oy* in *boy*, if pronounced with pursed lips (a more authentic parallel would be the Norwegian *øy*).

A Note on This Volume's Translations

The translations in this volume were prepared from the standard Old Norse texts edited by Guðni Jónsson and Bjarni Vilhjálmsson in *Fornaldarsögur Norðurlanda*, vol. 1 (Reykjavík: Bókaútgáfan forni, 1943). I have also used Guðni Jónsson's chapter names and mostly followed the chapter divisions printed there, while occasionally dividing chapters a sentence earlier or later. Decisions about punctuation (including quotation marks), capitalization, and the divisions of the Old Norse text into sentences and paragraphs are my own and reflect natural breaks in the narrative as perceived by a reader accustomed to English prose. The Old Norse text vacillates between the present and the past tense in narration, but I have regularized all narration into the past tense, and I have freely translated the conjunctions between clauses and sentences to insure an unmonotonous rhythm and style in English.

Where the Saga of the Volsungs quotes poems also preserved in the Poetic Edda, I have drawn the verses from my translation, *The Poetic Edda: Stories of the Norse Gods and Heroes* (Hackett, 2015).

Further Reading

Barnes, Michael, and Anthony Faulkes. *A New Introduction to Old Norse.* 3 vols. Viking Society for Northern Research, 2008.

> The most accessible and complete resource for anyone who wants to learn the Old Norse language.

Cook, Robert (translator). *Njal's Saga.* Penguin Classics, 2002.

> The most famous of the genre of sagas known as Sagas of Icelanders, a moving and violent tale of revenge in early Iceland.

Crawford, Jackson (translator). *The Poetic Edda: Stories of the Norse Gods and Heroes.* Hackett, 2015.

> The Poetic Edda preserves older and often different versions of many of the same stories about the heroes of the Saga of the Volsungs, especially Sigurd and Gudrún, and its poems were known and frequently quoted by the saga's author. The Poetic Edda is also the most important source for the myths of the Norse gods, including Óðin, Thór, and Loki.

Edwards, Cyril (translator). *The Nibelungenlied*. Oxford University Press, 2010.

The *Nibelungenlied* is an epic poem in Middle High German that tells a parallel but often strikingly different version of the story of the heroes of the Volsung and Gjukung families, set in the feudal chivalric world of medieval Germany.

Edwards, Paul, and Hermann Pálsson (translators). *Seven Viking Romances*. Penguin Classics, 1986.

A collection of seven sagas of mythical heroes, of a similar genre to the two in this volume. The sagas of Arrow-Odd and King Gautrek are particularly famous Viking adventures.

Haymes, Edward R. (translator). *The Saga of Thidrek of Bern*. Garland, 1988.

A sprawling, medieval Norwegian saga, which includes a very different form of the legend of Sigurd. A form of this saga probably influenced parts of the Saga of the Volsungs (for instance, chapter 23 of the Saga of the Volsungs appears to be modeled on chapter 291 of the Saga of Thidrek of Bern).

Kellogg, Robert (introduction), and various translators. *The Sagas of Icelanders*. Penguin Classics, 2001.

A collection of sagas of the genre called Sagas of Icelanders, featuring *The Saga of the People of Laxardal*, which is a rich narrative of medieval Iceland filled with allusions to the Saga of the Volsungs.

Ringler, Dick (translator). *Beowulf: A New Translation for Oral Delivery*. Hackett, 2007.

A remarkably well-done translation of *Beowulf*, an Old English poem that relates the story of a dragon-slaying hero similar to the heroes of the sagas in this volume. The text of *Beowulf* directly references some of the Volsungs by name in a brief allusion.

Saxo Grammaticus (author), Karsten Friis-Jensen (editor), and Peter Fisher (translator). *Gesta Danorum (The History of the Danes), Volume I.* Clarendon Press, 2015.

> A work of medieval scholarship by the Danish historian Saxo Grammaticus, who died in approximately AD 1220. Book 9 includes Saxo's version of the story of Ragnar Loðbrók and his sons, and other books in this volume include versions of other myths related in Norse sources such as the Poetic Edda.

Snorri Sturluson (author) and Anthony Faulkes (translator). *Edda.* Everyman's Library, 1995.

> A translation not of the Poetic Edda but the Prose Edda, a work by Snorri Sturluson (1179–1241) that summarizes many of the same mythological traditions as the Poetic Edda, including a brief overview of the exploits of the Volsungs.

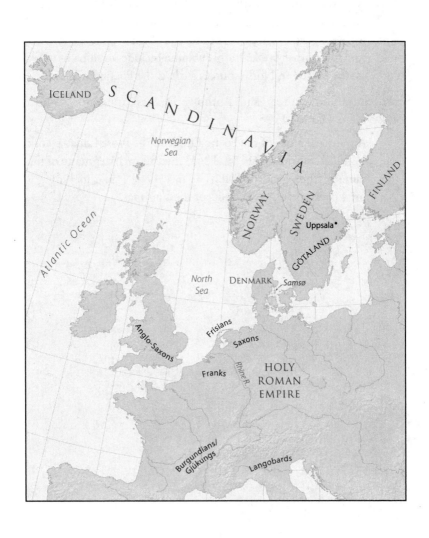

ICELAND

S C A N D I N A V I A

*Norwegian
Sea*

NORWAY

SWEDEN

FINLAND

Uppsala•

GÖTALAND

Atlantic Ocean

*North
Sea*

DENMARK   *Samsø*

Frisians

Anglo-Saxons

Saxons

Rhine R.

Franks

HOLY
ROMAN
EMPIRE

Burgundians/
Gjúkungs

Langobards

The Saga of the Volsungs
(*Volsunga saga*)

Chapter 1. Concerning Sigi, a Son of Óðin

Here begins the story of Sigi, who was said to be a son of Óðin. Another man named Skaði was also involved in this story. He was powerful and considered a great man, though between the two Sigi was more powerful and considered to be from a better family, according to the opinion of the time.

Skaði owned a slave who is somewhat worthy of being mentioned in this saga, whose name was Breði. He was wise in such matters as concerned him. He was as talented and accomplished as many men who were considered his betters, and perhaps even more so than some such men.

It is said that one day Sigi went hunting, and Skaði's slave Breði went with him. They hunted all through the day and into the evening. And when they collected their kills at the end of the day, Breði had killed not only more but better animals than Sigi. Sigi did not approve of this at all, and he said it was a strange thing that a slave outshone him in a hunt. He ran at the slave and killed him, and buried his body in a snowdrift.

Sigi went home that evening and said that the slave Breði had ridden away from him in the forest: "And he soon got out of sight, and I don't know where he's gone."

Skaði doubted Sigi's story; he suspected that it was a lie, and that Sigi had killed his slave. Skaði had his men search for Breði, and they found his body in the snowdrift. Skaði said that this snowdrift ought to be called a "Breði-drift" from then on. Ever since, people have taken after his example, and they call large snowdrifts by this name.

It was clear that Sigi had murdered the slave Breði. Sigi was declared an outlaw, and he could not remain at home with his father any longer.

Óðin traveled with Sigi a long way away from that land, never leaving him until he reached some warships.

Now Sigi went on raids with an army that his father Óðin gave him before they parted, and he was victorious in many battles. And it turned out well for him, and he was able to claim a land and kingdom for himself. He married well and became a great and powerful king and a mighty warrior, and he ruled Hunland. He had a son he named Rerir, who grew up in his father's kingdom and who was already a large and accomplished man at a young age.

Chapter 2. Concerning Rerir and His Son Volsung

Sigi grew old. He had many enemies, and he was betrayed by those he trusted most, his wife's brothers. They ambushed him when he least expected it, when he had only a few men with him. In the ensuing struggle, Sigi and all the bodyguards with him were killed.

Sigi's son Rerir was not there when his father was killed. When his father died, Rerir assembled a great number of his friends and local chieftains, and in their presence he claimed his father Sigi's land and kingdom for himself. And once he felt that his claim to the kingdom was secure, Rerir remembered what he owed to his uncles for killing his father. He assembled a large army and went to fight his uncles, since he thought that they had betrayed him so severely that their kinship was now invalid. For this reason he did not give up until he had killed all his father's killers, even though such a slaughter of near relatives had until then been unheard of in every way. He then took possession of all his uncles' lands and kingdoms and riches, and Rerir became an even greater man than his father had been.

Rerir now had plenty of treasure, and a wife who he thought suited him. Nevertheless, they were together a long time without producing a son to be Rerir's heir. Both of them were unhappy about this, and they prayed earnestly to the gods and asked them to grant them a child.

Frigg heard their prayer, and she told Óðin what they asked for. He was not in any doubt about how to help, and he sent one of his Valkyries, who was named Hljóð, a daughter of the giant Hrímnir. He gave the Valkyrie an apple and told her to give it to the king. She took the apple and turned into a crow, and flew into Rerir's kingdom and found him where he sat on a burial mound. She dropped the apple on his lap. He picked up the apple and thought he had an idea of what its significance might be. He went home and met with his queen, and ate a little of the apple.

The queen discovered shortly afterwards that she was pregnant, but the pregnancy lasted an unusually long time while she remained unable to give birth to the child.

Eventually it happened that Rerir went to battle, as kings often do in order to secure peace in their country. While he was away, he became sick and died of his illness. He intended to go to Óðin, which was thought to be desirable in his time.

The queen remained pregnant the same way without being able to give birth to the child, and this continued for six years. After six years of pregnancy, she believed she could not live much longer, and she gave orders to cut her open, and this was done.

The child was a boy, and as expected, he was already very big when he was born. It is said that the boy kissed his mother before she died.

The boy was given the name Volsung, and he became the king of Hunland after his father Rerir. He grew big and strong at a young age, and he was very bold in every kind of deed that requires manliness and courage. He became a very great warrior, and he was victorious in his battles.

When Volsung was full-grown, the giant Hrímnir sent him his daughter Hljóð, who has been mentioned before as the Valkyrie who brought Rerir the apple. He married her, and they were together a long time and had a good marriage.

Volsung and Hljóð had ten sons and one daughter. Their oldest son was named Sigmund, and their daughter was named Signý. They were twins, and both of them were the foremost and the most beautiful in every way of the children of King Volsung. All of Volsung's children were great, as has been told in stories for a long time, and it has become a famous tale that they were extremely proud and were the greatest of all those mentioned in ancient sagas, the greatest in wisdom and in all sports and all kinds of combat.

It is said that King Volsung ordered a magnificent hall to be built, with a large oak that stood in the middle of the floor with its branches and beautiful blossoms weaving among the beams in the roof, and its trunk standing in the middle of the hall. They called this tree Barnstokk.

Chapter 3. The Marriage of Siggeir to Signý, Volsung's Daughter

Siggeir was the name of the king who ruled over Götaland, and he was a powerful ruler with a large following. King Siggeir went to meet with King Volsung and asked Volsung for the hand of his daughter Signý. Volsung thought well of Siggeir's proposal, and so did his sons, though Signý herself was not eager to marry Siggeir. Nonetheless she let her father have his way in this, as she did in all matters concerning her. And her father thought it was advisable for her to marry Siggeir, so she was engaged to him.

And at the time when the wedding and wedding-feast were to be held, Siggeir was to come as a guest into Volsung's hall. King Volsung prepared the feast in the best possible manner, and when everything was ready on the appointed day, the guests came, including King Siggeir, and many noble men came with King Siggeir. It is said that many fires burned within, all along the length of King Volsung's hall, and at the center was the apple tree [sic] which has been told of before.

Now it is told that while the guests were seated around the fires during the feast, a man came into the hall. No one recognized this man. He was dressed in this way: he had a spotted cloak draped over himself, he was barefoot, and he had linen pants tied to his legs. He had a wide-brimmed hat on his head, and he was very tall, elderly, and had only one eye. This man drew a sword, and then he stabbed it into the tree trunk and it sank up to the hilt.

No one greeted this man. Then the man spoke: "Whoever draws this sword out of the tree trunk will receive the sword as a gift from me, and he will say truly that he never held a better sword in his hand than this one." And then the old man left the hall, and no one knew who he was or where he went.

Now all the men stood up, and they did not hesitate to try to take the sword, since they thought that the man who took it first would be its rightful owner. So the highest-born men went to the sword first, followed by all the others. No one who grasped the sword could pry it loose in any way. But then Sigmund, Volsung's son, came to try the sword, and it came out in his hands as if it had sat there loose for him. This weapon seemed so good to everyone that no one thought he had ever seen a sword so good, and King Siggeir offered to buy the sword from Sigmund for three times its weight in gold. But Sigmund said, "You could have taken this sword from the tree just as easily as I did, if it had been meant for you. But now, because it came to me, you will never receive it from my hand, even if you offer me all the gold you own."

King Siggeir was angry and thought he had received a mocking reply. Yet because he was a man of underhanded character, he behaved as though he didn't care about the sword at all, but during that evening he thought up the revenge that he would later carry out.

Chapter 4. Siggeir Invites Volsung to Visit Him

Now it is told that King Siggeir went to bed that same night with his bride Signý. The next day the weather was good, and Siggeir said he would like to go home and not wait for the wind to worsen or the sea to become unpassable. It is not told that Volsung or any of his sons hindered him, especially because Volsung could tell that Siggeir wanted more than anything to depart from the feast.

Signý told her father, "I don't want to go away with King Siggeir. There is nothing in my heart that smiles for him. And I know, thanks to my gift of second sight which is common in our family, that this decision will cause a disaster for us if you won't change your mind immediately."

"You ought not to talk this way, daughter," said Volsung, "because it would be an enormous shame both to him and to us to break this agreement, with Siggeir innocent of wrongdoing. And we would lose all his trust and friendship if we broke the marriage agreement, and he would pay us back with as much harm as he could, and the only proper thing for us to do is to honor our end of the agreement."

Now King Siggeir prepared to leave for home. But before he left the feast with his bride, he invited his father-in-law King Volsung and his sons to visit him in Götaland in three months' time, and to bring as many warriors as he wished and who would do him credit with their company. King Siggeir wanted to do this as repayment for the shortened wedding-feast, as it was not the custom to do as he had done, leaving the wedding feast after only one night.

King Volsung promised to make the journey and to meet Siggeir at his home on the agreed day. Then father-in-law and son-in-law parted, and Siggeir went home with his bride.

Chapter 5. Concerning the Treachery of King Siggeir

Now it is told that King Volsung and his sons went at the agreed time to Götaland at the invitation of King Siggeir, Volsung's son-in-law. They had three ships, all of them well-equipped. The journey went well and they came to Götaland late in the evening.

That same evening Signý came to her father King Volsung and asked to speak with him and her brothers in private. She told them about Siggeir's plans, including the fact that Siggeir had assembled an unbeatable army and he intended to betray them. "Now I beg you," she said, "that you return to your kingdom and gather the largest army you can, and then come back here and avenge yourselves. Do not walk into this trap, because you won't fail to be betrayed if you don't do as I ask."

Then King Volsung said: "Everyone will say that I swore, while still in my mother's womb, that I would never flee in fear from iron nor from fire, and I have kept that oath all of my days until now—and why would I not keep it in my old age? And no women will mock my sons, saying that they feared to die. Everyone will die someday, and no one can escape death when his time has come. I say that we will not flee but will do everything we can in the boldest way. I have fought in a hundred battles, sometimes with the larger army and sometimes with the smaller, and yet I have always had the victory. It will never be said that I fled, nor that I begged for peace."

Signý wept miserably and asked Volsung not to send her back to King Siggeir. But King Volsung answered, "You will absolutely go home to your husband and stay with him, whatever happens to us."

Signý went back to her husband, and Volsung and his sons remained there overnight. And in the morning when it dawned, King Volsung ordered all his men to stand up, leave their ships for the land, and prepare themselves for battle. They all went ashore fully armed, and it was not long before King Siggeir arrived with his entire army, and the ensuing battle was extremely hard and the king aggressively urged his men forward. And it is said that on this day, King Volsung and his sons went all the way through the ranks of King Siggeir's army eight times, cutting with weapons in both hands. And when they were preparing one more such assault, King Volsung fell dead in the middle of his own troops. And there all of his men fell, except for his ten sons, because there was much more opposition from the enemy than they could overcome. All of his sons were captured, tied up, and led away.

Signý was aware that her father had been killed, and that her brothers were captives destined for death. She called King Siggeir to her for a private conversation, and she said, "I wish to request that you not kill all my brothers immediately, but instead have them held captive in the stocks. I recall that it is said that 'An eye loves what it lingers on,' and I will not ask for anything more, as I don't expect it would be granted to me."

King Siggeir answered, "You are foolish, and senseless, to request that your brothers be tormented more than if they were simply decapitated. But I will grant your request, because I'll like it better if I subject them to worse, and make them suffer longer in dying."

Now Siggeir ordered it to be done as Signý had requested. A huge tree trunk was taken and laid lengthwise over the legs of the ten brothers at a particular place in the forest, and they sat there all day until nightfall. And at midnight there came an old she-wolf, huge and ugly, to the place where they were pinned down by the tree trunk. Each night she would tear one of them to death with her teeth, and then eat him entirely, before she went away.

The morning after, Signý sent a trusted servant to her brothers, to find out what the news was. And when the messenger came back, he reported that one of her brothers was dead. She was despondent at the thought that they would all die this way, with her unable to help them.

There is little more to tell. Nine nights in a row, the same wolf came at midnight and killed and ate one of the brothers, until only Sigmund was left alive. But before the tenth night fell, Signý sent her trusted servant to Sigmund. She gave the servant honey, and told him to spread it all over Sigmund's face and to leave some in his mouth. Then the servant went to Sigmund and did as he was told, and returned home.

That night, the wolf returned according to her usual habit, intending to kill and eat Sigmund as she had done to his brothers. But when she smelled him, she noticed the honey, and she licked his whole face with her tongue and then stuck her tongue into his mouth. Sigmund's courage rose up, and he bit down on the wolf's tongue. She sprang back hard and struggled mightily, and braced her feet against the tree trunk with such strength that it burst apart. Sigmund held on to the wolf's tongue with his teeth so hard that the tongue was torn out of the wolf's throat at the root, and the wolf died of this injury.

Some say that this wolf was the mother of King Siggeir, and that she had taken a wolf's form by the use of magic and sorcery.

Chapter 6. How Sigmund Killed the Sons of Siggeir

Now the stocks where he had been trapped were destroyed, and Sigmund was free, and he remained there in the forest. Signý sent messengers to find out what had happened, and whether Sigmund still lived. When the messengers came to where Sigmund was, he told them everything that had happened with the wolf and his brothers. They went home and reported the situation to Signý.

Then Signý went and met her brother, and they agreed that he ought to build himself a house out of earth in the forest. A long time passed while Signý hid him there, and she brought him whatever he needed.

For his part, King Siggeir believed that all the Volsungs were dead.

Siggeir and Signý had two sons, and it is told that the oldest was ten years old when Signý sent him to meet Sigmund. She intended for the boy to help Sigmund if he tried to avenge their father Volsung.

The boy went into the forest, and late in the evening he came to the turf-house Sigmund lived in. Sigmund greeted him well and appropriately, and asked the boy to make bread for them. "And I will get us firewood," said Sigmund. Sigmund gave him a bag with flour and left to look for firewood.

But when Sigmund came back, no baking had been done. Sigmund asked if the bread was ready. The boy said, "I didn't dare touch the flour bag, because there's something alive in there." So Sigmund thought that this boy might not be brave enough that he'd like to have the boy with him.

When Sigmund and Signý next met, Sigmund told Signý that he didn't feel like a man was near him, no matter how near the boy was. Signý said, "Then kill him. He doesn't need to live any longer." And Sigmund did so.

A winter passed, and the next winter Signý sent her younger son to meet Sigmund. But there is no reason to dwell on that story for long, because it went the same way, and Sigmund killed the boy at the request of Signý.

Chapter 7. The Origin of Sinfjotli

It is now told that Signý was sitting in her room one time when a very powerful witch visited her. Signý said to her: "I would like for the two of us to switch our forms."

The witch answered, "That's for you to decide." And so the witch used her magic to cause the two women to exchange shapes. The witch sat in Signý's room in place of Signý, as Signý requested, and in the evening she went to bed next to King Siggeir. And the king did not discover that it was not Signý next to him.

Now Signý went to where her brother lived in the turf-house, and she asked for lodging for the night "because I'm lost in the forest, and I don't know where I am."

He said that she could stay there, as he wouldn't deny hospitality to a woman traveling alone, and he didn't expect her to repay his generosity with betrayal. So she came into the house and they sat down and ate. Sigmund's eyes were often drawn to the woman, and he thought she was truly beautiful. And when they had finished eating, he told her that he wanted them to share one bed that night. She said nothing against this, and Sigmund laid her down on his bed three nights in a row.

After this, Signý went home and met the witch again. She asked that they exchange looks once again, and they did so.

And after some time passed, Signý gave birth to a boy, and he was given the name Sinfjotli. And as Sinfjotli grew up, he proved to be big and strong and good-looking, and very much of the Volsung type. He was not yet ten years old when Signý sent him to Sigmund in his turf-house.

Before she sent them to Sigmund, Signý had tested her and Siggeir's sons by sewing the sleeves of their shirts to their arms, through skin and flesh. They had taken it badly and complained about it. Now she did the same to Sinfjotli, and he did not react. Then she ripped the sleeve from his arm, so that the skin came off with it. She admitted that this must put him in a lot of pain.

"Volsung wouldn't have thought much of such an injury," he said.

Now Sinfjotli came to Sigmund, and Sigmund asked him to make bread while he went to get firewood. He handed him the bag of flour, and went into the woods. And when he came back, Sinfjotli was finishing his baking.

Sigmund asked Sinfjotli if he had found anything in the bag of flour.

"I am not without suspicion," said Sinfjotli, "that there was something alive in the flour, when I started kneading the dough. But I kneaded it down, whatever it was."

Then Sigmund laughed and said, "You can't eat this bread tonight. You've ground down a huge poisonous serpent in it."

Sigmund was so powerful that he could eat poison without being harmed, but Sinfjotli could not eat or drink poison, though he could endure poison that fell on his skin.

Chapter 8. The Vengeance of the Volsungs

Now the saga tells that Sigmund thought Sinfjotli was too young to avenge Volsung with him, and he wanted to get Sinfjotli accustomed to some hardship first. They went out during the summers, traveling widely through the forests and killing men for their money. Sigmund thought Sinfjotli was much like a man of the Volsung kin, though he believed that Sinfjotli was King Siggeir's son, and thought that he had his father's evil disposition even if he had the vigor of a Volsung. He also thought Sinfjotli had a certain contempt for his family, because he often reminded Sigmund about the wrongs he had suffered and often encouraged him to kill King Siggeir.

One time, the two of them went into the forest to go robbing, and they found a house where two men were sleeping who wore thick golden rings. These men were princes who had suffered an evil fate, because wolfskins hung over them in the house and they could only come out of these wolfskins every tenth day. Sigmund and Sinfjotli put the wolfskins on and could not remove them. Like the princes before them, their voices were also changed into wolves' howls, although they both understood each other.

Now they took to the forests, each one on his own path. They made an arrangement that one of them would risk his life to attack up to seven men on his own, but not more than seven, and to howl for the other if he were in danger. "Let's not break this arrangement," said Sigmund, "because you're young and full of daring, and men will think it's good to hunt you."

Now each of them went his own way. And one time when they were apart, Sigmund came across seven men and let out a howl. When Sinfjotli heard it, he ran to Sigmund immediately and killed all the men, and they separated once again.

And when Sinfjotli had not wandered a long way into the forest, he encountered eleven men and fought them, and he killed them all. But he was badly injured himself, and he went under an oak tree and rested there. He did not have long to wait for Sigmund, and they talked together for a while. Sinfjotli said to Sigmund, "You had help killing seven men, but I'm a child in age next to you, and I didn't ask for help killing eleven."

Sigmund leapt at him so hard that Sinfjotli lost his footing and fell, and Sigmund bit into his throat. That day they were unable to come out of their wolfskins. Sigmund took Sinfjotli up on his back and carried him home to the turf-house. There he sat over Sinfjotli and cursed the wolfskins, saying the trolls could take them.

One day Sigmund watched two weasels fighting, and one of them bit the throat of the other. Then the weasel ran into the forest and got a leaf that he put on the other one's wound, and the wounded weasel stood up unharmed. Sigmund then saw a raven flying with a leaf, and the raven gave it to him. He put the leaf on Sinfjotli's wound, and Sinfjotli sprang up unharmed as if he had never been injured.

After this they went into Sigmund's turf-house and stayed there until it was the tenth day and they could take off the wolfskins. Then they took the skins and burned them and cursed them, saying they would never cause anyone harm again.

During this time of bad fate, they did many brave things in King Siggeir's land. And now Sinfjotli was a grown man, and Sigmund thought that he had tested him plenty.

Now a short time passed before Sigmund wanted to see to avenging his father, if it could be done. And he and Sinfjotli left their turf-house one day and came to King Siggeir's house and went into the entryway in front of the hall, where there were beer barrels, and they hid themselves there. Queen Signý knew where they were and wanted to see them. And when they met, they all agreed to a plan, that Sigmund and Sinfjotli would take their vengeance when night fell.

Signý and Siggeir had two young children who were playing on the floor with gold pieces. They rolled the gold pieces around the hall and ran after them. And when one golden ring rolled out of the house to the place where Sigmund and Sinfjotli were, one of the boys ran after it, and he saw where two large and grim-looking men were sitting wearing tall helmets and shining coats of armor. The boy ran back into the hall to his father and told him what he had seen, and the king suspected that there might be some treachery at hand.

Signý heard what was said. She stood up, took both the children and went out into the entryway to Sigmund and Sinfjotli and told them that they ought to know that the children had betrayed them. "And I advise you to kill them," she said.

Sigmund said, "I will not kill your children, even if they've betrayed me." But Sinfjotli did not hesitate; he drew his sword and killed both the children, and threw them into the hall at the feet of King Siggeir.

The king stood up and called to his soldiers to seize these men who had been hiding in his home that evening. Some men ran out and seized them, but Sigmund and Sinfjotli defended themselves manfully and well, and the man who had it worst was whoever stood closest to them. But finally they were overwhelmed and captured and tied up and put into chains, and then they sat there the whole night.

Now King Siggeir pondered what kind of death he could give them that would be slowest. And when morning came, the king had a big burial mound made of stone and turf, and when this mound was ready, he had a large flat stone set in the middle in such a way that one end of the stone stood up, and the other down. This stone was so large that it could barely be circled by the arms of two men standing on either end. Now he had Sigmund and Sinfjotli set into the mound on either side of this stone, because he thought it would be worse for them to be separated even though they could hear one another.

And when the workers began to fill the mound back in, Signý came with a bundle of straw in her hands and threw it into the mound with Sinfjotli, and she ordered the slaves not to tell King Siggeir about this. They obeyed her, and finished closing the mound.

And when night fell, Sinfjotli said to Sigmund, "I don't expect we'll lack food for a while. Queen Signý has thrown a side of bacon into the mound for us, and wrapped it up in straw." And then he felt the meat more closely and found that Sigmund's sword was sheathed inside it, and he found the hilt, and told Sigmund. Both of them celebrated. Now Sinfjotli stabbed up through the earth above the stone and cut hard. The sword bit into the stone. Then Sigmund took the point of the blade in hand and the two of them together sawed through the stone until it was split in half, as the poem tells:

> They cut that great stone
> with their strength.
> Sigmund wielded the sword,
> and Sinfjotli did as well.

And now they were both free to move around in the burial mound, and they cut through stone and iron and escaped.

Now they walked to King Siggeir's hall, where everyone was asleep. They stacked up wood by the hall and set fire to it, and the people inside woke up to the smoke inside and the hall burning over them. King Siggeir asked who had set the fire.

"Here I am with Sinfjotli, my nephew," said Sigmund, "and now we think that you ought to know that not all the Volsungs are dead."

Sigmund asked Signý to come outside and receive praise and great honor. He said that he wanted to compensate her this way for her miseries.

But she answered: "Now you will see whether I have remembered the murder of King Volsung by King Siggeir. I had our children killed, when I thought they were too slow to avenge our father, and Sigmund, I went to you in the forest disguised as a sorceress, and Sinfjotli is your and my son. He is exceedingly manly, because he is the son of both a son and a daughter of Volsung.

"Everything I have done has been to bring about the death of King Siggeir my husband, and now I have done so much to accomplish my vengeance that I cannot choose to live. I ought to die now with King Siggeir by choice, as I lived with him by force." Then she kissed her brother Sigmund and Sinfjotli and she went back into the fire and wished them farewell. There she died with King Siggeir and all Siggeir's followers.

Sigmund and Sinfjotli got an army and ships, and Sigmund set a course for his ancestral home and drove out the king who had set himself up there after King Volsung. Sigmund now became a great and powerful king, both wise and well-advised, and he married a woman named Borghild. They had two sons, named Helgi and Hámund.

And when Helgi was born, the Norns came to him to determine his fate, and they said that he would become the most famous of all kings. Sigmund had come back from a battle, and he gave his son a clove of garlic and the name Helgi, and as his naming-gift he added the lands of Hringstaðir and Sólfjoll and a sword, and he urged him to do great things and to be a Volsung.

Helgi became great and popular, and better than most other men at every kind of skill, and it is said that he rode to battle while still only fifteen years old. Helgi was made king over the army, and Sinfjotli came with him and they both commanded the troops.

Chapter 9. Concerning Helgi, Killer of Hunding

[compare *Helgakvida Hundingsbana (Helgakvitha Hundingsbana) I* & *II* in the *Poetic Edda*]

It is said that Helgi met a king in battle who was named Hunding. He was a powerful king with a large army, and he ruled many lands. A battle erupted between them, and Helgi pushed forward hard, and the battle ended with Helgi taking the victory. King Hunding fell, together with a large part of his army. Now Helgi was thought to have become a greater man, since he had killed such a powerful king.

Hunding's sons wanted to avenge their father, and they called out an army to oppose Helgi. They had a hard battle, and Helgi went through the troops of those brothers and sought out the sons of King Hunding and killed these: Álf, Eyjólf, Hervard, and Hagbard, and he claimed a great victory.

And when Helgi left the battlefield, he found several noble-looking women near a forest, and one of them was by far the most magnificent. They rode with excellent saddles and tack. Helgi asked the name of the foremost of them, and she told him her name was Sigrún, and that she was the daughter of King Hogni.

Helgi said, "Come home with us, and be welcome."

Sigrún said, "We have other work to do besides drinking with you."

Helgi said, "What is that, princess?"

She said, "King Hogni has promised me to Hodbrodd, the son of King Granmar, but I have answered that I would no sooner marry Hodbrodd than a nestling crow. But it will happen, unless you forbid him and come against him with an army and take me away, because there is no king I would rather share a home with than you."

"Be cheerful, princess," said Helgi, "I would rather put my boldness to the test than see you married to him, and we will see which one of us men is killed, and I pledge my life to this."

After this Helgi sent men with gifts to gather soldiers and assemble his army at Raudabjargir. And there Helgi waited until a great army came to him from Hedinsey, and then a great number of troops came to him from Norvasund with large, beautiful ships. King Helgi called to his captain, who was named Leif, and asked him if he had counted their troops. Leif said, "My lord, it is impossible to count all the ships that have come out of Norvasund. But there are 14,400 men on them, and another half as many elsewhere."

Then King Helgi said they should go into the fjord that was named Varinsfjord, and they did. A great storm came up and the waves surged so high that the sound of them hitting the decks was like the sound of boulders crashing together. Helgi told his men not to fear and not to reef the sails, but to set them all even higher than before. They were very nearly in danger of drowning before their ships could come to land. Then the princess Sigrún, daughter of Hogni, came riding on the land above and directed them to a good harbor called Gnípalund.

The men on land saw all this. And Granmar, who was the brother of King Hodbrodd and governed the region there at Svarinshaug, came riding on the land above. He called to them and asked who led this great army.

Sinfjotli stood up with a helmet on his head that was as reflective as glass, and a coat of chainmail that shone like snow, and a spear in his hand with a noble flag on it, and a gold-bordered shield held before him.

Sinfjotli knew how to talk to kings. "Tell them," he said, "after you've fed your pigs and dogs and found your wife, that the Volsungs are here, and in this army you'll find King Helgi, if Hodbrodd wants to encounter him. And it is Helgi's delight to fight boldly while you stay by the fire kissing serving-women."

Granmar said, "You don't know how to speak honorably or recall old stories, when you mock noble-born men with lies. It would be truer to say that you've lived a long time off wolves' food out in the wilds, and that you've killed your own brothers, and it's strange that you dare to travel with an army of good men when you've often sucked a cold corpse for its blood."

Sinfjotli said, "You must not remember clearly when you were the witch-woman on Varinsey and said that you wanted a husband—and chose me to be that husband. And then later you were a Valkyrie in Ásgard, and the men there almost all came to blows for your sake. I fathered nine wolves with you in Láganes; I was the father to each of them."

Granmar said, "You know how to tell plenty of lies. I don't think you could be anyone's father, considering that you were castrated by the daughters of the giant at Thrasnes. And you're the stepson of King Siggeir, and you dwelled in the forest with wolves and later all kinds of bad fortune came to you. You killed your own brothers, and made yourself a bad reputation."

Sinfjotli said, "Do you remember when you were the mare of the stallion Grani, and I rode you at the race in Brávellir? Later you were the goatherd of the giant Gaulnir."

Granmar said, "I would rather feed your corpse to the ravens than talk with you any longer."

Then King Helgi said, "It would be better, and wiser, for you two to fight than to talk like this, saying things that are shameful to hear. Granmar's sons are not my friends, Sinfjotli, but they are tough men."

Granmar then rode away, and met with King Hodbrodd at Sefafjoll. Their horses were named Sveipud and Sveggjud. They met by the cliff and Granmar told him his story. King Hodbrodd was in his armor and had a helmet on his head. He asked who these men were, and why they were so angry.

Granmar said, "The Volsungs have come here, and they have 14,400 men on land and 8,400 on the island called Sok. But they have their largest force at the place called Grindr, and I think that Helgi wants a fight."

King Hodbrodd said, "Let's send a message throughout the whole kingdom and fight them. Let no one who wants to fight sit at home! Let's send word to the sons of Hring, and to King Hogni and old Álf. They are great warriors."

The armies met at a place called Frekastein, and there was a hard battle there. Helgi pushed forward through the troops and there was a great loss of men. Then they saw a huge group of shieldmaidens, and to look upon them was like gazing into a flame. Princess Sigrún was there. King Helgi matched off with King Hodbrodd, and Helgi killed him there beneath the banners.

Then Sigrún said, "Have my thanks for this valiant deed. His lands are now yours. This is a very joyful day for me, and you will receive great fame and praise for having killed such a great king."

King Helgi took that realm as his own and lived there a long time. He married Sigrún and became a great and famous king, but he does not feature further in this saga.

Chapter 10. The Death of Sinfjotli

[compare *Frá dauda Sinfjotla (Fra dautha Sinfjotla)* in the *Poetic Edda*]

The Volsungs went home now, and they had greatly increased their fame.

Sinfjotli went out raiding anew. He saw a beautiful woman and wanted very much to have her. He asked for the hand of this woman, and so did the brother of Borghild, who was Sigmund's wife. The two men fought a battle over the woman, and Sinfjotli killed the other man, and then he went back to raiding everywhere and had many battles and always took the victory. He became the greatest and most famous of men, and he came home during the fall with many ships and a great deal of loot.

Sinfjotli told his father Sigmund the news, and Sigmund told his wife. She told Sinfjotli to leave their kingdom and said that she never wanted to see him again. But Sigmund said he would not drive Sinfjotli away, and he offered to pay Borghild with gold and great treasures, even though he had never before compensated anyone for a killing, because he said there was no prestige in arguing with women. She had no way to press the matter further, and said, "You ought to decide, my lord, as is proper."

With the permission of King Sigmund, Borghild hosted a funeral feast for her brother. She prepared the feast with all the best delicacies, and invited many great men.

Borghild served the drinks. She came before Sinfjotli with a great drinking horn and said, "Drink now, stepson."

He took the horn, looked in it, and said, "The drink is cloudy!"

Sigmund said, "Let me have it then." And he drained it.

The queen said, "Why should other men drink your beer for you, Sinfjotli?" And she came with a second drinking horn and said, "Drink now," and also said many other belittling things.

He took the drinking horn and said, "This drink is tainted in some way."

Sigmund said, "Give it to me then."

Borghild came a third time with a drinking horn and told Sinfjotli to drink it, if he had the courage of a Volsung.

Sinfjotli took the drinking horn and said, "There is some poison in the drink."

Sigmund said, "Wet your mustache, son!" King Sigmund was extremely drunk, which is why he spoke this way. Sinfjotli drank it, and he fell dead immediately.

Sigmund stood up, and his sorrow nearly killed him. He took Sinfjotli's body in his arms and carried him to the forest. Finally he came to a fjord where he saw a man on a small boat. The man offered to ferry him over the fjord, and Sigmund accepted. The boat was too small to hold all three of them, and so the ferryman took Sinfjotli's body first, and Sigmund walked along the shore. But in the next moment, the boat and the ferryman disappeared.

After this, Sigmund went home. He banished his queen, and a little later she died. King Sigmund still ruled his realm and was thought to be the greatest champion and king in his time.

Chapter 11. The Death of Sigmund, Son of Volsung

Eylimi was the name of a rich and powerful king. His daughter was named Hjordís, the wisest and most beautiful of women. King Sigmund heard that if this woman was not his match, none would be, and he went to the home of King Eylimi. Eylimi prepared a great feast for Sigmund, with the provision that Sigmund did not come with an army. But messengers went between the kings saying that Sigmund came in friendship and without hostile intent. The feast was to feature all the best food and a large crowd. And everywhere King Sigmund went on his way, markets and other traveling conveniences were provided, until he finally came to the feast, and the two kings shared one hall.

King Lyngvi, son of Hunding, was also there at that feast, and he also meant to win Eylimi's daughter for his wife. Eylimi did not think that Lyngvi and Sigmund could both get what they had come for, and he expected hostility from the one who did not.

King Eylimi said to his daughter, "You are a wise woman, and I have declared that you will choose your own husband. Choose between these two kings, and my decision will support yours."

She answered, "This is a difficult decision for me, though I will choose the king who is most famous. That is King Sigmund, although he is getting old."

And so she was married to King Sigmund, and King Lyngvi went away. And each day the guests were served with better food and with more enthusiasm. And after that King Sigmund went home to Hunland

and King Eylimi, his father-in-law, went with him and looked after his kingdom.

But King Lyngvi and his brothers now assembled an army and went to attack King Sigmund, because they had always lost to him in matters big or small, and now this marriage loomed largest. They wanted to test themselves against the heroism of the Volsungs, and they came into Hunland and sent Sigmund a message. They did not wish to ambush him, and they believed that he would not flee.

King Sigmund agreed to come to the battle. He gathered an army and sent Queen Hjordís to the forest with a serving-woman and a great deal of treasure. She was there while the battle took place.

The Vikings leapt from their ships with an enormous army. King Sigmund and King Eylimi set up their banners and the trumpets were blown. King Sigmund gave orders to blow the horn that had belonged to his father, and this was the way he urged his men forward. Sigmund had a much smaller army than Eylimi.

A great battle now began, and though Sigmund was old, he fought hard and he was always at the front of his men. Neither shield nor armor could protect a man from him, and he went again and again into the army of his enemies on that day, and no one could see what the outcome would be of this battle between the two armies. Many spears and arrows were in the air. But Sigmund's family spirits protected him so that he was not injured, and no one could count how many men fell by his hand. Both of his arms were covered in blood up to the shoulders.

And when the fighting had continued for a while, a man appeared in the fray who was dressed in a long hat and a blue cloak. He had only one eye, and a spear in his hand. This man charged against Sigmund and hefted up the spear at him. And when Sigmund struck hard with his sword, he hit the spearshaft and his blade broke into two pieces.

Now the tide of the battle turned, and Sigmund's luck left him and much of his army was killed. Sigmund stopped even trying to defend himself, and he continued to urge his troops on. Now it went like the saying goes, that no one can compete against superior numbers. Both King Sigmund and King Eylimi, his father-in-law, fell in this battle. They were at the front of his troops, and most of Sigmund's men fell with him.

Chapter 12. Concerning Queen Hjordís and King Álf

King Lyngvi now came to the king's residence and meant to take Hjordís, but this was not to be, and he found neither the woman nor any treasure there. He went over the land and divided it among his own men, and thought that he had killed all the Volsungs and that he had nothing to fear from them any longer after this.

Hjordís walked among the fallen bodies the night after the battle and came to where King Sigmund lay. She asked if he had any chance of living.

He said, "Many live with little hope, but my luck has left me, so I will not let myself be healed. Óđin no longer wishes for me to draw my sword, since he has now broken it. I have fought battles while it pleased him."

She said, "Nothing would seem lost to me, if you were to be healed and you avenged my father."

King Sigmund said, "That is a task fated for others. But you are pregnant with a boy. Raise him well and carefully, and that boy will become the greatest and most famous of our family. Take good care also of my sword's fragments. A good sword can be made from them, which will be called Gram, and our son will carry that sword and do many great things with it which will never be forgotten. And his name will be spoken as long as the world lasts. Take heart from that. But now my wounds overcome me, and I go to visit our dead kinsmen."

Hjordís sat over him until he died and the sun came up. Then she saw where many ships had come to land. She said to her servant, "Let's exchange clothes, and you take my name and say you are the daughter of King Eylimi."

They did so. The Vikings saw the great carnage and saw where two women were running for the woods. They understood that great things must have happened here, and they leapt off their ships. The leader of these warriors was Álf, son of King Hjálprek of Denmark. He had sailed along the shoreline with his army and now they came upon this scene of carnage where they saw so many dead.

The king told his men to look for the women, and they did so. Then he asked the women who they were, and a strange thing happened, as the servant answered for them and told them about the fall of King

Sigmund and King Eylimi and many other great men, and who had brought it about. The king asked whether the women knew where King Sigmund's treasure was hidden.

The servant answered, "We probably know," and showed them to the treasure. And they found great wealth there, so much that none of the men thought he had seen so much in one place nor more jewels, and they carried it all to the ships of King Álf. Hjordís and her servant went with King Álf when he returned home to his realm and told of the fall of the most famous of kings. The king positioned himself at the stern of the ship, and the two women sat on the foremost bench on the deck. He spoke with them, and he placed great value on what they said.

King Álf now came home to his kingdom with a great treasure. He was the most accomplished of men. And when they had been home a short time, the Danish queen asked her son King Álf, "Why does the more beautiful woman have fewer rings and worse clothing? It seems to me that the higher woman is the one you have treated lower."

He answered, "I have suspected that she did not act like a servant, and when we first met she showed that she knew how to greet well-born men. I will test this."

And now one time when they were drinking, the king sat and talked with the women and said, "How do you know that it is dawn, when the night draws to a close, if you cannot see the sun and stars?"

She answered, "This is our way of knowing. It was our custom in my youth that we drank a great deal in the hour before dawn, and even after I stopped this, I still wake at the same time, and that is my way of knowing."

The king smiled at this and said, "That was a bad habit for a king's daughter." Then he found Hjordís and asked her the same question. She answered, "My father gave me a small golden ring with this feature, that it would get cold in the hour before dawn on my finger. That is my way of knowing the dawn."

King Álf answered, "There was plenty of gold around, if even the servants had some! You women have hidden it from me for a long time, but I would have treated you as if we were both born of one and the same king, if you had told me, and I will give you even better honors, because you will be my wife. I will pay the brideprice once you have given birth to your child."

She answered, and told him that everything he said was true. She was given great honor there, and was considered the most noble of women.

Chapter 13. Concerning Sigurd and Regin

It is now told that Hjordís gave birth to a boy, and the boy was brought to King Hjálprek. Hjálprek was glad when he saw the boy's fierce eyes, and he said that the boy would be neither like nor equal to any man, and he was sprinkled with water and given the name Sigurd. Everyone says that there was no match for Sigurd anywhere, whether in achievements or in size. And when all the most excellent men and kings are listed in the old sagas, Sigurd is named before all of them for his boldness, his warrior spirit, his energy, and his drive, which he possessed beyond all other men in the northern half of the world.

Sigurd was raised there with King Hjálprek and greatly loved. He grew up, and every child loved him. Sigurd gave Hjordís to King Álf to be his bride and stipulated the brideprice to be paid for her.

Regin was the name of Sigurd's foster-father; he was the son of Hreidmar. He taught him sports, games, and runes, and how to speak many languages, as was fitting for a king's son, as well as many other things. One time when they were both together, Regin asked Sigurd if he knew how much wealth his father had owned or who might have kept it. Sigurd answered that the kings Hjálprek and Álf had it.

Regin asked, "Do you trust them completely?"

Sigurd said, "It's fitting that they keep it until I need it, because they can guard it better than I can."

Then Regin came to talk to Sigurd a second time and said, "It's strange that you just want to be some stableboy for these kings and go around like a vagabond."

Sigurd said, "It isn't that way at all. I make decisions together with them. And what I want isn't kept from me."

And Regin said, "Then ask King Álf to give you a horse."

Sigurd said, "He will do it right away if I ask." So Sigurd went to see King Álf and King Hjálprek.

One of them asked Sigurd, "What do you want?"

Sigurd said, "I'd like a horse to ride for fun."

King Álf said, "Then choose a horse for yourself, and whatever else you want that is ours."

The next day Sigurd went to the forest and met an old man with a long beard who was a stranger to him. The man asked Sigurd where he was going. Sigurd said, "I'm on my way to pick out a horse. Help me decide which one."

The man said, "Let's go and drive them into the river called Busiltjorn." So they drove the horses into the deepest part of that river, and all the horses swam out again except for one. Sigurd picked this one. He was a young gray stallion, big and handsome, and he had never been ridden before.

The old man said, "This horse is descended from Sleipnir. He should be brought up well, because he will be a better horse than any other." Then the man disappeared. Sigurd named the horse Grani, and he was indeed the best of all horses. The old man he had met was Óðin.

Soon Regin said to Sigurd, "You don't have enough money. It troubles me that you run around like some peasant's child, but I know of a way you could probably win some treasure, and it's even more likely that you would be honored and spoken of well if you got it."

Sigurd asked where this treasure was and who guarded it.

Regin said, "His name is Fáfnir, and his home is not far from here at a place called Gnitaheid. And when you see it, you will be sure to say that you have never seen more gold in one place, and you would never need more even if you became the oldest and most famous of all kings."

Sigurd said, "I have heard of this dragon, even though I'm young. And I have heard that no one dares come near him because of his huge size and evil nature."

Regin said, "That is not true. His size is within the normal range for snakes, and only rumor has made him out to be larger. Your esteemed ancestors would have thought so. And though you may be of the Volsung bloodline, it doesn't seem that you have their ferocity, since the Volsungs are considered the foremost of all in courage."

Sigurd said, "It may be that I don't have much of their boldness or quickness, but you don't have to make fun of me, since I'm still practically a child. Why do you want this done so badly?"

Regin said, "There's a story behind it, and I will tell it to you."
Sigurd said, "Let me hear."

Chapter 14. Concerning the Payment for Otter

[compare *Reginsmál (Reginsmal)*, st. 1–12, in the *Poetic Edda*]

"The beginning of this story is that my father was named Hreidmar, and he was an important and wealthy man. He had a son named Fáfnir, and a second one named Otter, and I was the third and the least of all three in terms of achievements and reputation. But I knew how to work with iron and silver and gold, and I made something new out of everything.

"My brother Otter had different habits and traits. He was a great fisherman, much better than other men, and he spent his days in the form of an otter, always in the river catching fish in his mouth. He would take his catch to his father, which was a great help to him. He was much like an otter, coming home late and always eating alone and with his eyes closed because he could not stand to see his food becoming less.

"And Fáfnir was by far the biggest of us and the cruelest, and he wanted to claim everything that there was for himself.

"There was also a dwarf named Andvari," continued Regin, "he was always in the waterfall that is called Andvari's Falls, in the form of a pikefish. He fed himself there, as there was an abundance of fish near the waterfall. My brother Otter often went to Andvari's Falls and caught fish in his mouth and set each one afterwards on the land.

"One day Óðin, Loki, and Hønir were traveling and they came to Andvari's Falls. Otter had caught a salmon, and he was eating it on the riverbank with his eyes closed. Loki threw a stone and killed him. The Æsir felt very lucky about this and skinned the otter and made a bag out of the skin. That same evening they came as guests to Hreidmar's house and showed him what they had caught. We captured them and threatened their lives if they did not fill that bag with gold, and cover it on the outside with gold as well. Then the Æsir sent Loki to acquire the gold. He came to Rán and borrowed her net, and went back to

Andvari's Falls and threw the net in front of the pikefish, and the fish jumped in. Then Loki said:

> "'What kind of fish is this
> swimming in the water,
> that doesn't know to avoid a net?
> Your head will stay
> on your body, if you
> can get me some gold.'

> "'I am named Andvari,
> son of Óin,
> I have been in many waterfalls.
> A cruel Norn
> shaped my fate at the beginning,
> cursed me to live in the water.'

"Loki saw all the gold that Andvari owned. And after he had taken all of it, Andvari still had one single ring, and Loki took that from him as well. The dwarf then hid inside a stone and said that this ring and the gold would cause the death of everyone who owned it.

"The Æsir gave Hreidmar the gold. They filled the otter-skin with gold and set the skin on its feet, so that they could cover it with gold from the outside. And when this was done, Hreidmar reached forward and saw one whisker that was still visible, and told the Æsir to cover it. Ódin took the ring Andvaranaut and covered the whisker with it. Then Loki said:

> "'The gold is delivered.
> We've paid a huge price
> for my head.
> I do not foresee
> happiness for your son.
> This gold will be the death of you both.'

"Then Fáfnir killed his own father," continued Regin, "in cold blood, and I got none of the treasure. He became so evil that he slept outside and allowed no one to enjoy the treasure except himself. Soon he turned into the worst kind of serpent and rested there on the treasure. Then I went to the king and became his smith. And this is the end of my story, that I missed out on compensation both for my brother and my father. And ever since then, gold has been called 'payment for the otter,' and this is the reason."

Sigurd said, "You have been through a terrible loss, and your kinsmen have been very evil. Now make a sword with your cunning skill, a sword with no equal, so that I can perform great deeds if my courage serves me, and if you want me to kill this great dragon."

Regin said, "I will make it, and trust that you will kill Fáfnir with it."

Chapter 15. Regin's Sword-Craft

Now Regin made a sword and gave it to Sigurd. Sigurd took the sword and said, "This is your sword-craft, Regin," and swung it at the anvil. The sword broke. He threw it away and told Regin to make a better one.

Regin made a second sword and gave it to Sigurd. Sigurd looked at it, and Regin said, "This one will be to your liking, though you're a hard man to work for." Then Sigurd tested this sword, and it broke like the first one.

Sigurd said to Regin, "You're going to be like your earlier kinsmen and prove untrue." Then he went to see his mother. She greeted him well, and they took to talking and drinking. Sigurd said, "Have I heard correctly that King Sigmund gave you the sword Gram in two pieces?"

She said, "That is true."

Sigurd said, "Give it to me. I want to have it."

She said he was likely to win fame, and she gave him the sword.

Now Sigurd went to Regin and asked him to make as good a sword as he could make from these fragments. Regin became angry and went to his shop with the fragments and thought Sigurd was being very presumptuous about his work.

Now Regin made another sword. And when he took it from the furnace, it seemed to his apprentice as though flames were flickering from its blade. Regin asked Sigurd to accept this sword, and he said that he did not know how to make a sword at all, if this one failed. Sigurd swung it at the anvil and cut it in two down to the base, but the sword was neither broken nor chipped. Sigurd praised the sword and went to the river with a tuft of wool and threw it in against the stream, and the wool split in two when it touched the swordblade. Sigurd went home happy.

Regin said, "You'll keep your promise, now that I have made the sword, and you'll fight Fáfnir."

Sigurd said, "I will keep my promise, but first I will avenge my father."

As Sigurd continued to grow up, he grew more beloved by everyone, and every child loved him completely.

Chapter 16. Sigurd's Meeting with Grípir

[compare *Grípisspá (Gripisspa)* in the *Poetic Edda*]

Grípir was the name of a man, Sigurd's maternal uncle. Soon after the sword had been made, Sigurd went to meet with him, because Grípir could see the future and he knew men's fates beforehand.

Sigurd asked Grípir how his own life would go. Grípir hesitated a long time but finally answered Sigurd's eager request to tell his whole fate, in exactly the way that it would later turn out. And when Grípir had said these things, as he was asked, Sigurd rode home.

Soon after this he met Regin, who said, "Kill Fáfnir, as you swore to do."

Sigurd said, "I will keep my promise, but first I will avenge my father King Sigmund, and my other kinsmen who fell in battle with him."

Chapter 17. Sigurd Avenges His Father

[compare *Reginsmál (Reginsmal)*, st. 13–26, in the *Poetic Edda*]

Now Sigurd went to the kings Álf and Hjálprek and said, "I have been here a while, and I owe you both love and great honor. But now I wish to leave and find the sons of Hunding, and I want them to know that not all the Volsungs are dead. I would like to have your support in this."

The kings said that they would give him everything he asked for.

Now a great army was assembled and outfitted well with ships and armor so that Sigurd would travel even more honorably than before. Sigurd captained one longship which was the longest and best of all. The sails were beautifully fashioned and impressive to see. They set sail with a favorable wind, but when a few days had passed, a huge storm came upon them, and the sea was like blood to look upon. Sigurd did not order his men to reef the sails, even though they were ripping, but instead he ordered them set even higher.

And when they sailed past a certain peninsula, a man called up to the ship and asked who was in charge of this fleet. He was told that Sigurd Sigmundsson was their chieftain, and that he was the foremost of all young men.

The man said, "Everyone says the same thing about him, that there is no king's son to equal him. I would like you to take in the sails on one of those ships and let me have a ride."

They asked him what his name was, and the man replied:

> "They called me
> Battle-Stirrer,
> when young Volsung
> set a table for the ravens.
> You can call me
> 'Man on the Rock,'
> or 'Burden' or 'Spellcaster.'
> I want a ride."

They went to land and the man came aboard, and the weather immediately improved. They sailed until they came to land in the realm of King Hunding's sons. Then Spellcaster disappeared. They attacked the land with fire and iron, killing men and burning towns, and destroying every place they visited. Some men escaped into the protection of King Lyngvi and told him that a great army had come to the land and was destroying everything and showing more ferocity than had ever been seen. They said that Hunding's sons had not been far-sighted when they claimed that they had nothing to fear from the Volsungs, since it was Sigurd Sigmundsson who led this army.

King Lyngvi sent a war summons all around his kingdom. He did not wish to flee, and he gathered every man to him who would give him his support, and together with his brothers he met Sigurd with a huge army. A supremely fierce battle erupted between them, and many spears and arrows could be seen in the sky. Axes were swung hard, shields were broken, chainmail was split open and helmets dented in, skulls were hacked apart, and not a few men fell dead to the earth.

And when the battle had gone on in this way for a long time, Sigurd went to the vanguard of his troops past his own flagbearers, and the sword Gram was in his hand. He killed men and horses alike, forcing his way through the enemy troops. Both his arms were bloody up to the shoulders. Men ran away wherever he turned, and neither helmet nor chainmail withstood him, and no one thought he had ever seen such a man before. The battle lasted a long time with severe casualties and savage fighting.

A rare thing happened there, that an aggressive army in its own homeland lost a battle. So many men fell in the army of Hunding's sons that no one could count them. Sigurd was always in the front of the fighting.

Now Hunding's sons came at Sigurd himself. Sigurd swung at King Lyngvi and split helmet, head, and armored body in one blow. Then he struck at Hjorvard, Lyngvi's brother, and cut him in two pieces, and then he killed all the sons of Hunding who had previously survived, along with most of their army.

Sigurd went home with a well-won victory and all the great treasure and praise he had won in this campaign. Great feasts were given in his honor in his homeland.

And when Sigurd had been home a little while, Regin came to him and said, "Now you'll want to bow Fáfnir's head, as you swore to do, because now you have finished avenging your father and your other kinsmen."

Sigurd said, "I will keep the promise I swore to you. It has not fallen out of my memory."

Chapter 18. Concerning the Slaying of Fáfnir

[compare *Fáfnismál (Fafnismal)*, st. 1–22, in the *Poetic Edda*]

Now Sigurd and Regin went up on Gnitaheid, and there they found the path that Fáfnir followed when he slithered down to the water. It is said that the cliff Fáfnir sat on when he drank from the water below was thirty feet high. Sigurd said, "Regin, you told me that this dragon wasn't any larger than an average snake, but the trail he's left here tells me he is very large."

Regin said, "So dig a pit and sit in it. And when the dragon comes slithering to the water, stab him in his heart and kill him that way. You'll win great fame for it."

Sigurd said, "What will happen to me if I get the dragon's blood on me?"

Regin said, "There's just no getting you to do anything, since you're afraid of everything. You are nothing like your departed kinsmen when it comes to courage." Then Regin fled in terror, and Sigurd rode up on Gnitaheid and dug a pit.

And while he was at this work, an old man with a long beard came up to him and asked what he was doing there. Sigurd told him.

The old man said, "This is unwise. Dig more pits, so that the blood will run off into them, while you sit in this one and stab the dragon's heart." Then the man disappeared, and Sigurd dug more pits, as the man had advised.

And when the dragon came slithering toward the water, there was an earthquake that shook all the earth in the vicinity. The dragon blew poison from his mouth in every direction in front of him, and Sigurd was afraid neither of the sight nor the sound. And when the dragon slithered over his pit, Sigurd stabbed him beneath his left armpit, so deep that the sword sank up to the hilt. Then Sigurd leapt up out of his pit and drew his sword back, and his arms were bloody up to the shoulders. And when the great dragon felt himself mortally wounded, he thrashed out with his head and tail and broke everything in reach.

And as Fáfnir felt himself dying, he said, "Who are you? Who is your father? What family are you from, that you were daring enough to bring weapons against me?"

Sigurd said, "No man knows my family. I am called 'clever beast,' and I have neither father nor mother. I am always alone."

Fáfnir said, "If you had no father and no mother, in what strange way were you born? And though you don't want to tell me your name on my death-day, you know that you're lying right now."

Sigurd said, "I am named Sigurd, and my father was Sigmund."

Fáfnir said, "Who convinced you to kill me, and why did you let yourself get talked into it? Did you never hear how everyone is afraid of me and my terror-helmet? You fierce-eyed young man, I don't doubt you had a warlike father."

Sigurd said, "My courage made me do it, and my strong hand helped, and this sharp sword which you felt inside you got it done. Not many men are brave in adulthood, if they were cowards as boys."

Fáfnir said, "I know, if you had grown up in your own family's embrace, you might have killed me for courage's sake. But it's a wonder that a captive taken in war was brave enough to fight me, because it's a rare prisoner who's bold in battle."

Sigurd said, "You mock me for being far away from my father's kin. But even though I was taken in war, I am no prisoner, and *you* noticed that I live free."

Fáfnir said, "You think that everything I say to you is mockery. But this gold I've claimed will bring about your death."

Sigurd said, "Every man will have control of his wealth until his fated death-day, but there is a time for each one of us to die."

Fáfnir said, "You don't want to hear my advice, but you will drown if you sail recklessly. Wait on the land, until you see the ocean calm."

Sigurd said, "Tell me, Fáfnir, if you are very wise: who are the Norns who choose which child gets which mother?"

Fáfnir said, "There are various different kinds of Norns. Some are god-born, some are elves, some come from the dwarves."

Sigurd said, "What is the name of the island where the gods and giants will fight their final battle?"

Fáfnir said, "It is called Óskapt." And then Fáfnir continued, "My brother Regin caused my death, and I laugh knowing that he'll cause yours, too. And that's what he wants.

"I wore a terror-helmet against all men as long as I sat on my brother's ransom, and I blew poison in every direction before me so that no man dared to come near me, and I feared no weapon. I never faced so many men that I did not still feel myself much stronger than they were, and everyone feared me."

Sigurd said, "That terror-helmet you speak of will not grant anyone victory. Every man finds, when he comes among his enemies at the start of a battle, that there is no bravest man."

Fáfnir said, "I advise that you take your horse and ride away from here as fast as you can. It's not unusual that a mortally wounded man still manages to avenge himself."

Sigurd said, "That's *your* advice, but I'll do something else. I'll ride to your lair and take the great treasure of gold that has been the property of your kinsmen."

Fáfnir said, "You will ride there, and find all the gold, and it will be enough for all your days. And that gold will kill you, and everyone else who owns it."

Sigurd stood up and said, "I'd ride home and leave this treasure alone, if I knew that I would never die. But every bold man wants to have control of his wealth until his fated death-day.

"And you, Fáfnir, lie there in your life's broken pieces, and may Hel have you." And with this, Fáfnir died.

Chapter 19. Sigurd Takes Fáfnir's Treasure

[compare *Fáfnismál (Fafnismal)*, st. 23–44, in the *Poetic Edda*]

After this Regin came to Sigurd and said, "Hail, my lord! You've won a great victory and killed Fáfnir. Before you, no one was brave enough even to sit in his path. Your bold adventure will be famous as long as the earth lasts."

But then Regin stood and looked down a long time. And then he said in great anger, "You have killed my brother, though I was not innocent in that crime."

Sigurd took his sword Gram and wiped the blood off the blade in the grass. He said to Regin, "You hid far away while I took a great risk and tested this sharp sword with my own hand. It was my strength that was tested against the dragon's, while you crept in the bushes and didn't know which way was up or down."

Regin said, "This dragon might have dwelled in his lair a long time if you didn't have the sword I made for you with my own hand, and then neither you nor anyone else would have accomplished this."

Sigurd said, "When men are in battle, a brave heart means more than a sharp sword."

Then Regin said in great anger, "You killed my brother, but I'm hardly innocent."

Now Sigurd cut the dragon's heart out with the sword named Ridil. Then Regin drank Fáfnir's blood and said, "Do me a favor, Sigurd, just a little favor. Take the dragon's heart to the fire and grill it, and then give it to me to eat."

Sigurd put the heart on a spit to grill it. And when the blood had boiled out of it, he put his finger to the heart to test whether it was fully cooked. He then put his finger in his mouth, and when the blood from the dragon's heart touched his tongue, he could understand the language of birds. He heard some wagtails talking in the branches above him.

One of the wagtails said, "There sits Sigurd cooking Fáfnir's heart. He ought to be the one who eats it, and then he would be wiser than any other man."

Another bird said, "Over there is Regin. He'll betray Sigurd, who trusts him."

A third wagtail said, "He should cut off Regin's head, and then all the gold would be Sigurd's alone."

A fourth one said, "He would be wiser if he took the advice you've given him, and rode to Fáfnir's lair and took all the gold there. Then he ought to ride up to Hindarfjall, where Brynhild sleeps. There he could learn great wisdom if he took your advice and thought about what he needed. I always suspect a wolf, when I see a wolf's ears sticking up."

A fifth said, "Sigurd isn't as wise as I thought, if he lets one brother live free when he has killed the other!"

A sixth said, "It would be very wise if Sigurd killed Regin and took all the treasure."

Sigurd said, "I won't stand for that poor fate, to be killed by Regin. I'd rather send both brothers in the same direction." Then he drew the sword Gram and cut off Regin's head.

Now Sigurð ate a part of the dragon's heart, and kept another part of it. Then he mounted up on his horse Grani and followed Fáfnir's tracks to his lair and found it open, and its doors were made of iron, as were the doorframes and all the pillars in the house, and they were dug deep into the earth. Sigurð found a great quantity of gold there and the sword Hrotti, and he took the terror-helmet and a golden suit of armor and many other precious treasures. He found so much gold there that he thought even two or three horses would hardly be enough to carry it. He took all the gold and put it into two large chests, and then he took his horse Grani by the bridle to walk him. The horse would not move and would not be driven along. Then Sigurð thought he knew what the horse wanted. He leapt on Grani's back and struck him with his spurs, and then the horse ran as if he carried nothing at all.

Chapter 20. Sigurð Meets Brynhild

[compare *Sigrdrífumál* (*Sigerdrifumal*), st. 1–20, in the *Poetic Edda*]

Sigurð rode a long way, until he rode up on the mountain Hindarfjall and turned to go south toward Frankish lands. He saw a great light on the mountain, as though a fire burned there, and it glowed against the sky. When he came to it, he saw a fortress, and there were flags flying on top of it. Sigurð went into the fortress and saw a person sleeping there on the floor, fully armed. He took the helmet off first, and then he realized this person was a woman. Her chainmail was as tight as if it had grown to her skin. He cut the chainmail off, first cutting down the middle, and then down both sleeves, and his sword cut as if through cloth. Then Sigurð told her she had been sleeping long enough.

She asked what had been powerful enough to break her chainmail. "And who woke me? Is it Sigurð Sigmundsson who has come, carrying Fáfnir's helmet and the sword that killed Fáfnir in his hands?"

Then Sigurð said, "I am a man of the Volsung family who has done this, and I have heard that you are the daughter of a mighty king. I have also been told of your beauty and wisdom, and I want to see them proven."

Brynhild said that two kings had fought. One was named Hjálm-Gunnar; he was old and a great warrior, and Óðin had promised him victory. The other was named Agnar, brother of Auði. "I killed Hjálm-Gunnar in this battle. But Óðin stung me with a sleep-thorn in revenge for this, and said that I would never again have victory in battle and that I would have to marry. But I swore an oath in response that I would marry no man except one who knew no fear."

Sigurð said, "Teach me some wisdom in important matters."

She said, "You know better, but I will teach you gratefully if there is anything I know that may please you about runes or any other sort of thing. Let us drink together, and may the gods give us a good day and grant that you find something useful and wise in my knowledge, and that you'll remember what you and I say."

Brynhild filled a cup and gave it to Sigurð, and then she said:

> "I bring you beer,
> warrior,
> blended with strength
> and fame.
> It's full of spells
> and magic,
> good enchantments
> and happy words.

> "You should carve victory-runes
> if you want to have victory.
> Carve some on the hilt of your sword,
> carve some on the middle of the blade also,
> some elsewhere on the sword,
> and name Týr twice.

> "You should make wave-runes
> if you want to save ships
> out on the wild water.
> You should carve them on the ship's bow
> and on the steering-rudder,
> and burn them into the oars.

Then there won't be any steep wave,
there won't be any blue waves,
that you won't escape from safely.

"You should learn speech-runes
to prevent those who hate you
from taking vengeance on you.
Wind them around,
weave them around,
set them all around,
at the court
where people go
for judgments.

"You should learn beer-runes
if you don't want another man's wife
to abuse your trust if you have a tryst.
Carve them on the drinking-horn
and on the back of your hand,
and carve the rune for 'N' on your fingernail.

"You should bless the drinking-horn;
then watch out for trouble
and throw garlic in the drink.
If you do this, I know
you'll never drink mead
that's blended with a curse.

"You should learn life-saving runes
if you want to save a woman's life
when she is in the throes of childbirth.
Carve them on your palm,
and clasp them around your limbs,
and pray to your family spirits for help.

"You should learn limb-runes
if you want to be a healer

and learn how to heal wounds.
Carve them on bark,
carve them on the needles of a pine
that bends eastward.

"You should learn mind-runes
if you want to be wiser
than any other man.
Óðin read them,
Óðin carved them,
Óðin thought them up.

"Runes were carved on the shield
that stood before the shining sun,
on the ears and hooves
of the horses that draw the sun,
on the wheel
of the chariot of Thór,
on the reins of Sleipnir,
on the reins of his sled.

"They were carved on a bear's paw
and a poet's tongue,
on a wolf's claws
and an eagle's beak,
on bloody wings
and a bridge's beams,
on a helper's palm
and a healer's footprint.

"They were carved on glass
and gold, on treasures,
in wine and in beer
and a witch's chair,
in a man's flesh
and Óðin's spearpoint
and a troll-woman's breast,

on a Norn's fingernail
and the beak of an owl.

"All of them that were carved
were then shaved off,
and they were stirred into the holy mead
and sent far away.
Some are with the Æsir,
some are with the elves,
some are with the Vanir,
and mortal men have some.

"The beechtree-runes
and life-saving runes
and all the beer-runes
and the famous strength-runes
will be of good use
for everyone who knows them
completely and correctly.
Use them, if you know them,
till the gods die.

"Now you must choose
from the options you are offered,
you lord of sharp weapons.
Choose to speak,
or choose to remain silent:
Your fate is already decided."

Sigurd responded:

"I will never flee,
even if you know I am doomed to die.
I was not born a coward.
I want to have
all of your loving advice,
as long as I live."

Chapter 21. Concerning the Counsel of Brynhild

[compare *Sigrdrífumál* (*Sigerdrifumal*), st. 21–37, in the *Poetic Edda*]

Sigurd said, "There has never been a wiser woman in all the world. Teach me more wisdom."

She said, "It's fitting that I do as you say and give you more good advice, both because you ask for it and because you are yourself wise." She continued, "Behave faultlessly with your kin. Don't avenge yourself on them, and bear their evils patiently, and you'll live a long life in reward.

"Beware of evil things, either the love of a girl or another man's wife. Bad things often come from them.

"Don't be seen with fools when you're in public. They often say worse things than they realize, and then you'll be called a coward and others will think that their slander is true. Wait for another day to kill the fool, and then repay him for his lie.

"If you go where evil spirits live, be careful. Don't sleep near the road, even if darkness is setting on you outside, because there are often evil spirits who dull men's minds living there.

"Don't let pretty women tempt you, even if you're at a party, because they'll keep you from sleeping, or else they'll make you miserable. And don't try to seduce them with kisses or with pretty words.

"If you hear drunk men saying something stupid, don't talk to them. They're drunk and their wits are gone. Such conversations will often cause sorrow or death.

"Fight your enemies right away. Never wait for them to burn you inside your own home.

"Never swear a false oath. Grim vengeance comes to oathbreakers.

"Respect a dead body, whether the death was from sickness, or drowning at sea, or from violence. Prepare the body carefully.

"You should never believe someone if you have killed his father, or his brother, or any other close relative of his, even if he is a young man. There's often a wolf that lurks in a dead man's young son.

"Beware of being deceived by your own friends.

"And I cannot see much of your future, if I am wrong in saying you can expect to be hated by your brothers-in-law."

Sigurd said, "I think there is no one wiser than you. I swear I will marry you, and you're a good match for me."

She said, "I would choose you even if I could choose from all men." And they sealed these words with oaths.

Chapter 22. Description of Sigurd, Killer of Fáfnir

Now Sigurd rode away. He carried a shield in a convex shape, and it was plated with pure gold with a design in the shape of a dragon set into it. The shield was charred dark brown on top but painted bright red at the bottom, and his helmet, saddle, and leather jacket were colored the same way. He wore a golden shirt of chainmail, and all his weapons were trimmed with gold, and on all his weapons was the design of a dragon, so that everyone who saw him who had heard the story would know that it was he who had killed the mighty dragon called Fáfnir by the Norse. And all of his weapons were trimmed in gold and colored chestnut brown because he was far above all other men in noble birth and courtly manners and in almost every other way. And when all the greatest champions and the most outstanding chieftains are counted, he will always be counted first, and his name is famous in all the languages spoken north of the Mediterranean, and it will be so as long as the world lasts.

Sigurd had chestnut-colored hair that flowed in beautiful long locks. He had a well-trimmed, thick beard of the same color. He had a high nose, a broad, big-boned face, and his eyes were so bright that there were few men who dared to look under his brow. He was so broad across the shoulders that it was like looking at two men. Every part of his body was big and tall and as good-looking as it could be. And it is a sign of his great height that when he carried his sword Gram in the scabbard at his belt—and the sword was three and a half feet long—if he happened to walk in a field of full-grown rye, then the bottom point of his scabbard would touch the top of the plants.

And Sigurd's strength was even greater than his size would suggest. He knew how to fight with a sword and how to throw a long or short spear and how to hold a shield, how to shoot an arrow and ride a horse, and he learned many other noble arts in his youth.

He was a wise man who could see the future before it happened, and he understood the language of birds, and because of talents like these there were few events that caught him by surprise.

He could give a good, long speech, and he was so clever with words that he could not begin to speak for some cause without convincing everyone who heard him, before he had finished, that there was no other way to see the matter. And his joy was in giving help to his men and in testing himself in great deeds, and in taking treasure from his enemies and giving it in turn to his friends. He had no lack of courage, and he was never afraid.

Chapter 23. Sigurd Stays with Heimir

Sigurd now rode until he came to a large town, which was ruled by the great chieftain named Heimir. Heimir was married to Brynhild's sister, who was named Bekkhild. She was named Bekkhild (*Hild* of the bench) because she stayed at home and learned women's arts while her sister was named Brynhild (*Hild* of the armor) because she went out to battle in helmet and armor. Heimir and Bekkhild had a son named Alsvid, the noblest of men.

Some men were playing outside, and when they saw the man riding into town, they stopped their game and marveled at the man because they had never seen his like. They went and greeted him well. Alsvid invited Sigurd to stay with him and to be served whatever he wanted, which Sigurd accepted. Everything was arranged so that Sigurd was served in magnificent fashion. Four men took the gold from his horse Grani, and another was assigned to take good care of Grani. They could see many precious and rare treasures among all the gold. They entertained themselves looking at the helmets and suits of chainmail and the big rings and the wonderfully large golden cups and the weapons of every kind.

Sigurd stayed there a long time in great honor. His famous deed of killing the horrible dragon had now become famous in every land.

These noblemen enjoyed themselves well, and they were loyal to one another. They enjoyed themselves by preparing their weapons and making arrows, and hunting with their hawks.

Chapter 24. Sigurd Meets Brynhild

At this time Brynhild, Heimir's foster-daughter, came home. She sat in a room with her serving-women, and she was more skillful with her hands than other women. She made a tapestry of gold and sewed into it scenes that depicted all of Sigurd's great deeds, the killing of Fáfnir and the winning of the treasure and the death of Regin.

It is told that one day Sigurd rode to the forest with his dogs and hawks and a large entourage. And when he came home, his hawk flew up high on a tall tower and sat beside a window there. Sigurd followed the hawk, and he looked through the window and saw that it was Brynhild within. Her tapestry impressed him as much as her beauty.

When he entered the hall, he had no interest in entertaining himself with the others there. Alsvid said, "Why are you so quiet? This mood saddens me and your friends. Why can't you be happy? Even your hawks are sullen and so is Grani, and we can hardly do anything to change it."

Sigurd said, "My good friend, listen to what I'm thinking. My hawk flew up on a high tower, and when I retrieved him, I saw a beautiful woman. She was sitting by a golden tapestry. I looked at it and saw my own past and future accomplishments."

Alsvid said, "You have seen Brynhild, daughter of Budli, who is the most talented of women."

Sigurd said, "That must be true. How long has she been here?"

Alsvid said, "She came at about the same time you did."

Sigurd said, "I know that was a few days ago. This woman seems better to me than any other woman in the world."

Alsvid said, "Don't dwell on one woman, such a man as you are. It's bad to brood over what you can't have."

"I'm going to meet her," said Sigurd, "I'll bring her gold, and she will give me joy and return my feelings."

Alsvid said, "In her whole life, there has never been a man she would sit next to or give a drink to. She wants to be a warrior and do famous deeds."

Sigurd said, "I don't know whether she'll answer me or not, or whether she'll let me sit next to her."

And the next day after, Sigurd went to Brynhild's room. Alsvid stood outside the room and made shafts for his arrows.

Sigurd said, "Hello, my lady. How do you do?"

She said, "I am well. My kinsmen and friends are alive. But there is a danger in the fate that every man carries until his death-day."

He sat next to her. Four women came in with large golden cups full of the finest wine and stood before them.

Brynhild said, "Few men, with the exception of my father, have been allowed to sit there."

He said, "It pleases me that this one is now allowed to."

The room was draped with the most expensive tapestries, and the whole floor was carpeted.

Sigurd said, "Now it has happened, as you promised me."

She said, "Be welcome here." Then she stood up with her four serving-women and she went to him with a golden cup and asked him to drink. He stretched out his hand for the cup and took her hand in his and sat her down next to him.

He embraced her neck and kissed her and said, "No woman more beautiful than you was ever born."

Brynhild said, "It is not wise to place your trust in a woman, because women always break their oaths."

He said, "The best day in my life would be the day I had you."

Brynhild said, "It is not our fate to live together. I am a shieldmaiden, and it is my place to wear a helmet among war-kings and assist them in their campaigns, and I am not afraid to fight."

Sigurd said, "We would be happiest if we lived together, and the pain of what you're telling me is harder to endure than sharp blades."

Brynhild said, "I will summon armies to battle, and you will marry Gudrún, the daughter of Gjúki."

Sigurd said, "No other princess tempts me, and I don't have any second thoughts about this. I swear before the gods that I will have you, or no woman otherwise."

She said likewise. Sigurð thanked her for this and gave her a golden ring, and they swore these oaths again, and he went away to join his men and he stayed there for a time and his joy was great.

Chapter 25. Guðrún and Brynhild Talk

A king was named Gjúki, who ruled south of the Rhine. He had three sons named Gunnar, Hogni, and Guttorm, and a daughter named Guðrún who was the most famous of women. All of his children were better than the children of other kings in every accomplishment, and in both beauty and size. His sons were always in battle, and they won many famous victories. Gjúki's wife was the witch Grímhild.

A king was named Buðli, who was more powerful than Gjúki although both were mighty kings. Buðli was the father of Brynhild and her brother Atli. Atli was the cruelest of men, big and black-haired and yet honorable and a great warrior.

Grímhild was a cruel-minded woman.

The rule of Gjúki and his sons was joyful, and mostly because of his children, who were so much better than everyone else.

One time Guðrún said to her serving-women that she was unhappy. One of them asked her what caused her unhappiness.

She said, "I had an unhappy dream, and now my heart is miserable. Interpret this dream that I will tell you."

The serving-woman said, "Tell me and don't be sad, because people always have dreams before storms come."

Guðrún said, "This is no storm. I dreamed that there was a beautiful hawk on my arm, with feathers made of gold."

The woman answered, "Many men have heard of your beauty, wisdom, and noble birth. Some king's son is going to come ask for your hand in marriage."

Guðrún said, "Nothing seemed better to me than this hawk, and I knew I would rather lose everything I owned than lose him."

The woman answered, "The man you marry will have noble manners, and you will love him well."

Guðrún said, "I'm upset that I don't know who he is, and I'm going to go meet with Brynhild. She will know."

Guðrún dressed herself in gold and beautiful clothing and traveled with her serving-women until they came to Brynhild's hall, which was decked with gold and stood on a high hill. And when people saw them coming, they told Brynhild that several women were coming in gilded wagons.

"It must be Guðrún, daughter of Gjúki," said Brynhild. "I dreamed about her last night. Let's go out and greet her. No women more beautiful are going to come visit me."

Brynhild and her serving-women went out and greeted Guðrún and her servants well. Then all of them went inside Brynhild's stately hall, which was richly decorated inside, and on the outside it was covered with a great deal of silver. Carpets were spread beneath their feet, and they were served well and played many kinds of games, but Guðrún was quiet.

Brynhild said, "Why can't you enjoy yourself? Don't be like this. Let's all enjoy ourselves together and talk about mighty kings and their great deeds."

"Let's do that," said Guðrún. "Who do you think has been the foremost of all kings?"

Brynhild said, "Haki and Hagbarð, the sons of Hámund. They have done many famous deeds in battle."

Guðrún said, "They were great and famous, though Sigar abducted their sister and burned other members of their family in their houses, and the brothers have been too slow to take vengeance. Why don't you mention my brothers, who many now consider to be the greatest of men?"

Brynhild said, "They come from a good family, but they haven't been tested much yet. And I know someone who is even better: Sigurð Sigmundsson. He was still only a child when he killed the sons of King Hunding, and avenged both his father as well as his mother's father Eylimi."

Guðrún said, "What is the story behind that? Are you saying that he was born when his father died?"

Brynhild said, "His mother went among the fallen after the battle and found King Sigmund wounded. She offered to treat his wounds, but he said he was too old to fight any longer and he told her to comfort herself with the knowledge that she was going to give birth to the noblest of sons, and this was a true prophecy in a wise guess. And after King Sigmund died she went with King Álf, and Sigurd was raised there in great honor, and he did many great things every day and he is the greatest man in the world."

Gudrún said, "You speak of him in love. But I came here to tell you my dreams, which have made me very miserable."

Brynhild said, "Don't be troubled by dreams. Spend your time with your family, who will make you cheerful."

"I dreamed," said Gudrún, "that I left my room with many other women and we saw a huge stag, much larger than other animals. His hair was made of gold. We all wanted to catch him, but only I managed to, and that stag seemed better to me than anything else could be. And then you shot down that deer right in front of me where I knelt. This was such a terrible grief to me that I could hardly bear it, and then you gave me a wolf pup, and it splattered me with the blood of my brothers."

Brynhild said, "I will tell you what is going to happen: Sigurd will come to you, the one I have chosen for my husband, and your mother Grímhild will give him a drink of cursed mead that will cause us all great conflict. You will be married to Sigurd, and then lose him shortly thereafter, and then you will be married to King Atli. Then you will lose your brothers, and then you will kill King Atli."

Gudrún said, "It makes me overwhelmingly sad to know these things." And then she and her serving-women went home to King Gjúki.

Chapter 26. The Marriage of Sigurd and Gudrún

Now Sigurd rode away with his great treasure, riding Grani with all his weapons of war and his other goods, and he parted with Alsvid in friendship.

Sigurd rode on until he came to the hall of King Gjúki. He rode into town and was seen there by one of the king's men, who said, "I think it's one of the gods who goes there. This man is covered all over with gold. His horse is much larger than other horses, and his weapons are amazingly beautiful. He is much more impressive than other men—this is the greatest of men, himself!"

King Gjúki went out with his guards and greeted his visitor and asked, "Who are you riding into our town, something no one would dare attempt except with the permission of my sons?"

He answered, "I am Sigurd, the son of King Sigmund."

King Gjúki said, "You are most welcome, and you are welcome to anything you might want here."

Sigurd went into the hall, and everyone there seemed short next to him. All of them served him food and drink, and he stayed there in great honor.

Sigurd rode together later with Gunnar and Hogni, Gjúki's sons, and though Sigurd exceeded them in all his accomplishments, they were all great men.

Grímhild noticed how much Sigurd loved Brynhild and how often he spoke of her, and she thought it would be better luck if he stayed with them and married her daughter Gudrún, since she saw that no one was Sigurd's equal, and she knew what a strong support he would be and that he had an incredible amount of wealth, far more than anyone had seen before. The king already treated him like another son, and their sons for their part gave him more honor than they gave themselves.

One evening when they sat and drank, Queen Grímhild stood up and went to Sigurd and greeted him and said, "Your presence here makes us joyful, and we wish to give you every kind of good thing. Take this horn and drink."

He accepted the horn and drank its contents completely.

Then she said, "King Gjúki will be your father, and I will be your mother, and Gunnar and Hogni will be your brothers when you swear oaths on this, and no one equal to the three of you will be found anywhere."

Sigurd took this gladly, and after he had drunk from the horn he forgot Brynhild.

Sigurd stayed there for some time. And one time Grímhild went to King Gjúki and placed her arms around his neck and said, "We have the greatest champion there ever will be in the world with us now. He would be a great ally to us. Marry him to your daughter, and give him a great treasure and whatever part of our realm he wants, and he will find joy living here."

The king said, "It is not often that a man offers his own daughters in marriage, but it is a greater honor to offer her to Sigurd than to have her courted by other men."

And one evening, when Gudrún served the drinks, Sigurd could see that she was a beautiful woman, and in every respect the most noble.

Sigurd stayed there for two and a half years with honor and friendship, and one day the king and his family spoke with Sigurd. King Gjúki said, "You have done me a great deal of good, Sigurd, and you have done much to strengthen my realm."

And Gunnar said, "I would do anything to see you stay here a long time, and would offer you both the kingdom and my sister, a prize no one else would get if he asked for her."

Sigurd said, "I am grateful for these honors, and I accept." And Sigurd, Gunnar, and Hogni swore an oath of blood-brotherhood, to act as if they were brothers by the same father, and a great feast was prepared that lasted for many days, and Sigurd was married to Gudrún. There were all kinds of joys and entertainments, and each day the service was even better than the last.

Sigurd, Gunnar, and Hogni traveled widely in many lands and did many great deeds, killing the sons of many kings. No one accomplished such great things as they did, and they returned home with huge quantities of loot.

Sigurd gave Gudrún some of Fáfnir's heart to eat, and this made her both crueler and wiser than she had been before. They had a son named Sigmund.

And one time Grímhild went to her son Gunnar and said, "You have great joy in ruling, except for one thing that you lack, which is a wife. Go and woo Brynhild. She would be a noble match, and Sigurd would ride with you."

Gunnar said, "She is certainly beautiful. And I am not reluctant to take this advice." He told this to his father and brothers and to Sigurd, and they were all eager to see it done.

Chapter 27. Sigurd Rides through the Ring of Fire

They prepared their journey carefully, and then rode over the mountains and valleys to King Budli, where Gunnar made his proposal. Budli said he would be in favor of the marriage, if Brynhild were not against it, because he said she was so proud that she would only be married to a man she wanted.

They rode now to Hlymdalir, and they were greeted well there by Heimir. Gunnar told him his errand, and Heimir said it would be Brynhild's choice about whether she would marry him or not. He added that her hall was not very far from his, and that she would only willingly marry a man who dared to ride through the burning ring of fire that rose in flames around her hall.

They found the hall and the fire around it, and they saw that the hall was roofed with gold and surrounded on all sides by fire. Gunnar was riding the horse Goti, and Hogni rode Holkvir. Gunnar rode toward the fire, but his horse balked.

Sigurd said, "Why do you balk, Gunnar?"

Gunnar said, "My horse won't leap over the fire," and then he asked if Sigurd would loan him Grani to ride.

"Of course," said Sigurd. And now Gunnar rode a second time at the flame, but Grani would not make the leap. And since Gunnar could not make his way through the fire, he exchanged appearances with Sigurd, as Grímhild had taught them to do. Then Sigurd rode Grani with the sword Gram in his hand and golden spurs on his feet. Grani leapt the flame when he felt the spurs.

There was a great roar as the fire surged, and the earth around them shook and the flames reached to the heavens. No one had dared to do this before, and it seemed as though he rode into darkness. Then the fire died down and he stepped off his horse into the hall. As the poem tells it,

> The fire surged,
> the earth shook,
> and the high flames
> sawed at the heavens.
> Not many kings
> were willing
> to ride that fire,
> nor step over it.
>
> Sigurd drove Grani
> with a drawn sword,

and the flames
withdrew before him;
the fire withered
for that man eager for honor.
Grani's harness, which once
had been Regin's, glowed.

And when Sigurd entered the flame, he found a lovely room and Brynhild sitting within. She asked who this man was, and he answered that he was Gunnar, the son of Gjúki. "And you are going to be my wife, with the consent of your father and your foster-father, provided you also agree, now that I have ridden through the burning ring of fire."

"I don't know how I'm going to answer this," she said.

Sigurd stood tall and leaned on his sword-hilt and said to Brynhild, "I will reward you with a great deal of gold and good treasures."

She answered with sadness, sitting in her seat like a swan on a wave, dressed in chainmail with a sword in her hand and a helmet on her head. "Gunnar," she said, "do not talk to me like this unless you are better than all other men and will agree to kill every other man who has ever asked to marry me, if you can be relied upon to do that. I have been in battle with the king of the Rus, and my weapons were red with blood, and I still long for such things."

He said, "You have done many great deeds, but now remember your oath that you would marry the man who rode over this flame."

She knew that this was a true reply, and she realized the importance of what he had said. She stood up and greeted him well, and he stayed there for three nights, sharing one bed with her, though he took the sword Gram and drew it from its sheath and placed it between them. She asked why he did this, and he answered that it had been foretold that this was how he would be married to his wife, or else he would die. Then he took the ring Andvaranaut, which he had given her earlier, off her finger, and gave her a new ring from Fáfnir's treasure. Then he rode out through the same fire back to his companions, and he and Gunnar exchanged appearances again and then they rode back to Hlymdalir and told what had happened.

That same day Brynhild went home to her foster-father Heimir and told him privately that a great king had come to her. "He rode through

my burning ring of fire, and he said he had come to propose to me and
that his name was Gunnar. And I said that Sigurd alone would do this,
and that I swore oaths to him on the mountain, and he was my first lover."

But Heimir said that everything would be done as agreed.

Brynhild said, "Áslaug, my daughter with Sigurd, will grow up here
with you."

And now Brynhild went to her father, and Sigurd and Gunnar rode
home. Grímhild greeted them well and thanked Sigurd for the service
he had done. A feast was prepared and a huge crowd attended. Then
King Budli came with his daughter Brynhild and his son Atli, and the
feast lasted several days. And when the feast came to an end, Sigurd
remembered all his oaths to Brynhild, but he said nothing.

Brynhild and Gunnar sat and were entertained, and drank
good wine.

Chapter 28. A Conversation between Gudrún and Brynhild

One day when the women went to the Rhine to bathe, Brynhild waded
further upstream from Gudrún. Gudrún asked why she acted this way.

Brynhild said, "Why would I act like your equal in this or anything
else? I think that my father is more powerful than yours, and my husband has done many magnificent things and he rode through the burning ring of fire, while your husband was the slave of King Hjálprek."

Gudrún answered angrily, "You would be wiser to keep your mouth
shut than to mock my husband. Everyone says that no better man, in
any respect, has ever come into the world, and it's not proper for you to
mock him when he was your first lover, and it was he who killed Fáfnir
and who rode through your fire when you thought it was King Gunnar.
And he lay in bed next to you and took the ring Andvaranaut from your
finger, and here it is for you to see."

Brynhild saw the ring and recognized it, and turned as pale as if she
had died. Then she went home and said nothing the whole evening.

And when Sigurd came to bed, Gudrún asked, "Why is Brynhild so
unhappy?"

Sigurd said, "I do not know for sure, but I suspect that we will soon know very clearly why."

Gudrún said, "Why can't she enjoy her wealth and happy company and the praise of everyone, when she married the man she wanted?"

Sigurd said, "Where was she when she said she was married to the best man, or the one she most wanted?"

Gudrún said, "I'll ask her in the morning what man she would most want to marry."

Sigurd said, "I don't recommend you do that. You'll regret it if you do."

But in the morning Gudrún and Brynhild sat in her room and Brynhild was silent. Gudrún said, "Be cheerful, Brynhild. Are you upset about what we said to each other? Or what keeps you from being happy?"

Brynhild said, "Nothing but malice makes you ask that. You have a cruel heart."

"Don't think that," said Gudrún. "Tell me."

Brynhild said, "You should only ask questions that you'll be better knowing the answers to. That's proper for high-ranking women. And it's good to be happy about good things, when everything is going as you like."

Gudrún said, "It's still too early to say if that's true, but there's something foresighted in what you say. What makes you angry at me? I did nothing to harm you."

Brynhild said, "You must pay for being married to Sigurd. I don't accept that you have a right to enjoy him or his great treasure."

Gudrún said, "I didn't know what you had said to him, and it was within my father's rights to arrange my marriage without your approval or presence."

Brynhild said, "What Sigurd and I said to one another was no secret, nor were our sworn oaths. You all knew that you were deceiving me, and you will pay for it."

Gudrún said, "You have a better husband than you deserve, but your jealousy will keep simmering, and many are going to pay for it."

"I could be content," said Brynhild, "if only you weren't married to the better man."

Gudrún said, "You have such a noble husband that I don't even know who a better king would be, and you have plenty of wealth and power."

Brynhild said, "Sigurd killed Fáfnir, and that is worth more than the whole kingdom of King Gunnar," or as the poem has it:

> "Sigurd killed the serpent,
> and that will not soon
> be forgotten by anyone
> while the world endures.
> But your brother
> dared neither
> to ride the fire
> nor to cross it."

Gudrún said, "Grani wouldn't cross the fire with Gunnar on his back, but Gunnar did dare to ride it, and there's no need to insult his courage."

Brynhild said, "I won't conceal that I have no love for Grímhild."

Gudrún said, "Don't insult her. She treats you like her own daughter."

Brynhild said, "She is the cause of all the evil that bites me. She gave the cursed beer to Sigurd so that he would forget even my name."

Gudrún said, "You are saying many untrue things, and that's a terrible lie."

Brynhild said, "Then enjoy Sigurd as if you hadn't deceived me. Your marriage is a mismatch, and the future will go with you as I foresee it will."

Gudrún said, "I'll enjoy him better than you wish, and no one thinks that Sigurd's too good for me, not in any way."

Brynhild said, "You speak callously, and you'll regret the words running out of your mouth. Let's not curse each other."

Gudrún said, "You spat all your curses out on me first and now you act like you want to make it better, but there's evil intent underneath."

"Let's stop this useless talk," said Brynhild. "I kept my mouth shut for a long time about the sorrow that lived in my heart, but I love only your brother. Let's talk about something else."

Gudrún said, "Your thoughts are hatching plans a long way in the future."

Terrible grief came from when those two women went to the river and Brynhild recognized Gudrún's ring, and from the conversation that ensued.

Chapter 29. Concerning Brynhild's Agony

After this talk Brynhild stayed in bed, and news came to King Gunnar that she was sick. He went to her and asked what was wrong, but she didn't answer and she lay as if she were dead. When he pressed her, she said, "What did you do with that ring I gave you, the one my father King Budli gave me the last time I saw him, when you and Gjúki came to him and promised to raid and burn unless he married me to you? Afterwards he came to talk to me and asked which man I would choose out of the ones who had come, and I said I would rather lead a third of the army and fight. I had two choices then, either to be married as he wanted, or to be without money and my father's good will, and my father said that his good will would be better for me than his anger. Then I thought about whether I ought to obey him or kill many men.

"But I thought it was unlikely that I could defeat him, and so I promised myself to the man who rode the horse Grani and had Fáfnir's treasure, the one who had ridden through my burning ring of fire and killed the men I asked him to. And no one had the courage to ride that fire except Sigurd alone. He rode the fire, he didn't lack the courage to do that. He killed the dragon and Regin and five kings—not you, Gunnar! You turned pale like a corpse, and you're no king and no champion. And I swore an oath, when I was at home with my father, that I would love only the best man ever born—and that is Sigurd! And now I am an oathbreaker because I'm not married to him, and for that I will cause your death. And I have evil to repay to Grímhild as well. There is no woman worse or more cowardly than she is."

Gunnar answered so that few could overhear, "You've said enough slander, and you're an evil woman for insulting a lady who's higher-ranked than you are, a woman who doesn't resent her lot in life like you do, or torment dead men or murder anyone, and she lives with praise."

Brynhild said, "I have done nothing secret and nothing wrong. My nature is otherwise. I would rather kill you." Then she tried to kill King Gunnar, but Hogni restrained her and put her in chains.

Gunnar said, "I don't want her to live in chains."

She said, "Don't worry about that. You'll never see me being cheerful in your hall again, nor playing games nor speaking happily, nor working good tapestries with gold nor dispensing good advice." And she said that her greatest grief was that she was not married to Sigurd. She stood up and struck her tapestry so that it broke apart, and then she ordered the doors to her room opened so that her miserable wailing could be heard a long way away. Her awful grieving could soon be heard all over town.

***

Gudrún asked her serving-women why they were so uncheerful and sad. "What is wrong with you? Why do you walk around like crazy people? What panic has come over you?"

Then one of them, a girl named Svafrlod, said, "It is an unlucky day, and our whole hall is filled with grief."

Gudrún said to her, "Stand up, we've slept long enough. And wake up Brynhild. Let's go back to our weaving and be cheerful."

"I can't do it," said Svafrlod. "I can't wake her up or even speak to her. She's drunk neither mead nor wine for many days. I think she's angered the gods."

And then Gudrún said to Gunnar, "Go and get Brynhild, and tell her I feel pity for her in her grief."

Gunnar said, "She has forbidden me from talking to her, or from touching her property." But then Gunnar went to see her and tried in many ways to get her to speak, without getting any response. He then went and found Hogni and asked him to see Brynhild. Hogni said he was not eager to do so, but he went, and he also got no answer from her. Then they met Sigurd and asked him to talk to her. He said nothing, and it stayed this way through the evening.

The day after, when Sigurd came home from hunting, he went to Gudrún and said, "I have a bad feeling that this grief is going to turn into something bigger, and that Brynhild is going to die."

Gudrún said, "My lord, many strange things happen where she is concerned. And she's slept for seven days and no one has dared to wake her up."

Sigurd said, "She isn't sleeping. She is preparing plots against us."

Then Gudrún wept and said, "It's a terrible feeling for me to know who your killer will be, Sigurd. But go and meet her and see if her pride is still swelling. Give her gold and see if that softens her anger."

Sigurd went out and found the door to Brynhild's room open. He thought she was sleeping, and he tore the sheets off her and said, "Wake up, Brynhild, the sun is shining in town and you've slept enough. Stop this gloominess and be cheerful."

Brynhild said, "What makes you so bold as to come see me? No one betrayed me worse than you did."

Sigurd said, "Why won't you speak to anyone? What's wrong with you?"

Brynhild said, "I will tell you the cause of my anger."

Sigurd said, "You've had your wits enchanted away if you think that I mean you harm. And you're married to the man you chose."

"No," she said. "It wasn't Gunnar who rode through the fire to me, and it wasn't Gunnar who came to me with a wedding gift of slaughtered enemies. I was perplexed by the man who came to my hall, I thought he had your eyes. But I could not see the truth because of the curse on my luck."

Sigurd said, "I am no better man than the sons of King Gjúki. It was they who killed the king of the Danes and King Budli's brother, a great chieftain."

Brynhild said, "I have so much evil to repay to them. Don't remind me of my sorrows. It was you, Sigurd, who killed the dragon and rode over the fire for my sake, and there were no sons of King Gjúki there."

Sigurd said, "I never became your husband nor were you my wife, and a good king bought the right to call you his bride."

Brynhild said, "The sight of Gunnar has never made my heart smile. I hate him, though I hide it for others' sake."

"It's monstrous not to love a king like him," said Sigurd. "What is it that bothers you the most? I would think his love would seem better to you than gold."

Brynhild said, "The worst of my miseries is that I can't think of a way to redden a bitter sharp sword in your blood."

Sigurd said, "Don't worry about that. It won't be long before some bitter sword does pierce my heart, and you won't have anything else to expect for yourself because you won't survive longer than I do. And I don't have many days left to live."

Brynhild said, "You talk like that because you hate me, and not just a little bit. But then you've cheated me out of all joy, and I care nothing for life anymore."

Sigurd said, "Live, and love King Gunnar and me. I'll give you everything I own if it will keep you from choosing death."

Brynhild said, "You hardly know my nature. You are better than all other men, and yet no woman seems more loathsome to you than I am."

Sigurd said, "It would be truer to say that I love you more than I love myself. But I was tricked too, and now that can't be changed, even though I regretted that you weren't my wife when I regained my memory. But I put up with what I had to when I was in this royal hall, and I was happy in spite of everything because we were all together. It may also be that things will go as the prophecies told, and if so I will not be worried."

Brynhild said, "You're telling me too late that you regret my misery. Now there is no repayment I will accept."

Sigurd said, "I wish that we could go into the same bed and you could be my wife."

Brynhild said, "Don't talk like that. I won't have two husbands under one roof, and I would rather die than betray King Gunnar." But then she remembered when she and Sigurd had met on the mountain, and the oaths they had sworn, and she said, "Now it's all ruined, and I don't want to live."

"I didn't remember your name," said Sigurd, "and I didn't recognize you until you had already been married to him, and that is my greatest misery."

Brynhild said, "I swore an oath to marry the man who would ride through my burning ring of fire, and I will either keep my oath or die otherwise."

"I would rather leave Gudrún and marry you, than see you die," said Sigurd. And his chest swelled with so much agony that his chain-mail burst.

"I don't want you," said Brynhild. "And I don't want anyone else."

And then Sigurd went away. As it says in the poem about Sigurd:

Sigurd left
after they talked,
that resolute
companion in battle,
his head drooped
and the sides
of his chainmail shirt
split open.

And when Sigurd came back to the hall, Gunnar asked if Sigurd had found out what the problem was with Brynhild, or whether she was speaking again. Sigurd said she could speak. And now Gunnar went to see her once again, and he asked what the point of all her unhappiness was, or if there might be some cure for it.

"I don't want to live," said Brynhild, "because Sigurd betrayed me, and he betrayed you no less when you let him sleep in my bed. I will not have two husbands at one time under one roof, and this will be the death of Sigurd or me or you, because he has told Gudrún everything, and she ridicules me."

Chapter 30. The Murder of Sigurd

[compare *Sigurdarkvida (Sigurtharkvitha)
en skamma*, st. 1–41, in the *Poetic Edda*]

After this Brynhild went outside and sat beneath the wall of her room and went over her misery again and again. She said that she hated everything, land and power alike, because she could not have Sigurd.

Gunnar continued to come to her. Brynhild told him, "You will lose everything you rule and everything you own, and you'll lose your life and you'll lose me, and I will go home downcast to my own kinsmen and remain there, unless you kill Sigurd and his son. Don't raise his wolf-pup."

Gunnar became despondent and was uncertain what he should do, since he had sworn oaths to Sigurd. But he thought often about what an unparalleled shame it would be if his wife divorced him.

Gunnar said, "I think Brynhild is better than all other women. She is the most famous of all women, and I would rather lose my own life than lose her love." He called then for his brother Hogni and said, "I am in a terrible dilemma."

He then told Hogni how he wanted to kill Sigurd, and how he thought Sigurd had betrayed his trust. "And we would have all his gold and the whole kingdom to ourselves," he added.

But Hogni replied, "It would be shameful to break our oaths with violence. He has been a tremendous support to us, and there is no set of kings anywhere who can equal us as long as the Hunnish king Sigurd lives. We'll never again have such a man for our brother-in-law. I think it's a very good thing to have such a brother-in-law, and his son, for an ally. But I know what started this. It is Brynhild who made you think murderous thoughts, and her advice will lead us to terrible humiliation and harm."

Gunnar said, "It will happen as I say, and I have a plan. Let's convince our brother Guttorm to do it. He is young and ignorant, and was too young to swear a pledge to Sigurd."

Hogni said, "This is an evil plan in my opinion. And if we go through with it, we will pay a high price for betraying a man like him."

But Gunnar said that Sigurd had to die, "or else I will." He then told Brynhild to stand up and be cheerful. She stood, but she said Gunnar would not come into the same bed with her until the murder was done.

Now the brothers made their plan. Gunnar said that Sigurd deserved death for being the man who had taken Brynhild's virginity. "And let's convince Guttorm to kill him," he added.

Gunnar and Hogni called Guttorm and offered him gold and vast lands if he would do it. They took a snake and some wolf-flesh and they cooked these and gave them to Guttorm to eat, as the poet says,

> They took snake-meat
> and wolf-meat
> and gave it to Guttorm,
> blended with beer
> and many other things
> in the enchanted drink.

And once this was done with the witchery of Grímhild, Guttorm became wild and aggressive and he swore to commit the murder, and his brothers vowed to give him great honor in reward.

Sigurd was unaware of this treacherous plan and knew no reason why he deserved such evil treatment, but he could not fight what fate had in store for him.

Guttorm went into Sigurd's room that morning and found him resting in his bed. But when he looked at him, he could not find the courage to attack him, and he ran back out, and then this happened a second time. Sigurd's eyes had such a serpent-like brightness that very few dared to look him in the eye. But when Guttorm came back in the third time, he found Sigurd asleep and Guttorm drew his sword and stabbed him and the point of the sword pierced the mattress beneath him.

Sigurd woke up when he was stabbed, and Guttorm started for the door. But Sigurd took up the sword Gram and threw it after him, and it struck him in the back and cut him in half at the waist. His hips and legs fell forward, and his head and arms fell backwards into the room.

Gudrún was asleep in Sigurd's arms when she woke in dumbstruck terror, soaked in her husband's blood. Then she screamed, weeping and raving, and Sigurd lifted his head from the pillow and said, "Don't cry. Your brothers are still alive and there is joy for you in that. And there is my young son, who cannot fight his enemies on his own, and they have done themselves harm with their actions. They won't find a better nephew or brother-in-law to ride with them in battle—if they let him grow up. And now it has happened as was long ago foretold, but I refused to believe. No one can fight his fate.

"Brynhild is the cause of this, because she has more love for me than for anyone, but I swear truthfully that I never did any wrong to Gunnar, and I respected the oaths we swore, and I was never too much of a friend to his wife.

"And if I had known this before, and had I been able to stand on my feet armed with my weapons, many men would have lost their lives before I fell, and then all your brothers would be dead, and I would be harder for them to kill than the biggest buffalo or wild boar."

And now King Sigurd died, and Gudrún screamed so that she lost her breath. Brynhild heard her and laughed, when she heard that scream.

Gunnar said to her, "You're not laughing like this because you're cheerful in the roots of your heart. Why have you turned pale? You're a murderous woman, and you're likely near your death. Nothing would be more fitting than to see your brother King Atli killed before your eyes, and you'll be the cause of that too. Now we have to see about the funeral of our brother-in-law, our brother's killer."

Brynhild said, "No one thinks that the murders are over, but King Atli doesn't care about your threats or angry words. He will live longer than you, and he'll remain a more powerful man."

Hogni said, "Now everything has happened as Brynhild said it would. This is an evil deed that we'll never be able to make right."

Gudrún said, "My brothers have killed my husband. And the next time you ride out to battle, you will find that Sigurd is not riding at your right hand, and you'll remember that he was your good luck and he was your support, and if he had lived to have sons like him you'd be the stronger for his children and kinsmen."

No one could explain why Brynhild had laughed when she asked them to do it, and wept when it was done.

Chapter 31. The Death of Brynhild

[compare *Brot af Sigurdarkvidu (Brot af Sigurtharkvithu)*, st. 15–19, *Sigurdarkvitha en skamma (Sigurtharkvitha en skamma)*, st. 34–71, and *Helreid Brynhildar (Helreith Brynhildar)* in the *Poetic Edda*]

Brynhild said, "Gunnar, I dreamed that I slept in a cold bed, and you rode into the hands of your enemies. You and all the Niflungs will be cursed, you oathbreakers!

"You must have forgotten when you and Sigurd blended your blood in a pledge of brotherhood, and that it was your idea. Now you have repaid all his good with your evil—Sigurd, who let *you* be the foremost.

"When he came to woo me, I tested how faithfully he would keep his promises. He laid a sharp-edged sword between us, hardened with poison.

"It didn't take much to convince you and your brothers to do harm to him and me. I once lived at home with my father and had everything I wanted, and I wanted to marry none of you when you three kings came riding to our home. But my brother Atli asked me if I wanted to marry the man who sat on Grani's back. And that man did not resemble you in any way, and I promised myself to that son of King Sigmund and to no other.

"And your luck, Gunnar, won't improve, even if I die."

Then Gunnar rose up and he touched his wife's neck and begged her to live and accept money, and everyone else begged her to live, too. But she drove away everyone who came to her, and said she would not be talked out of what she planned on doing.

Gunnar went to Hogni and asked his advice, begging him to go to Brynhild and find out if anything could be done to soften her anger. Gunnar said that there was great need, that her mind needed to be changed and there wasn't much time to do it.

But Hogni said, "Let no one try to talk her out of killing herself. She's been no good to us or to anyone else since she came here."

And now Brynhild ordered a huge amount of gold to be brought to her, and she invited everyone to come and take it who wanted any. Then she took a sword and put it through her own heart and sank down by her bed and said "Everyone who wants it, take some of the gold now." But they were all silent. And again she said, "Take the gold as my gift and enjoy it."

Then Brynhild spoke again to Gunnar. She said, "Now let me talk to you for a little while about what is going to happen. You will make peace with Guðrún, with the assistance of Grímhild's magic. Guðrún will give birth to Sigurd's daughter, named Svanhild, and she will be the most beautiful woman ever born. Then Guðrún will be married unwillingly to my brother King Atli.

"Gunnar, you will want to marry my sister Oddrún, but Atli will forbid it. But the two of you will still meet in secret, and she will love you, and Atli will betray you and he will put you inside a snake-pit, and soon after Atli and his sons will be killed at Guðrún's hands. Then the ocean's waves will take Guðrún to King Jónakr's castle, and she will give birth to his excellent sons. And then Svanhild will be married off to King Jormunrekk, but Bikki's advice will be the cause of her death. And with that, your family will come to an end, and Guðrún's agony will be all the worse.

"Now, Gunnar, I make my last requests. Make a great funeral bonfire on the flat plain for all of us, for me and Sigurd and the men who were killed with Sigurd. Put a blood-reddened tent above it, and burn me on one side of that Hunnish king. And burn my men on the other side of him, two at his head and two at his feet, and burn two hawks. Then everything will be arranged properly.

"And between him and me, place Sigurd's drawn sword, just as it was the last time we shared a bed, when we pledged to become husband and wife.

"And it won't be as if the door was just shut on Sigurd's heels this way, if I follow him, and our funeral won't be remembered like some peasant's passing if you kill five slavewomen and the eight slavemen my father gave me to follow him, and burn them there along with the men who were killed with Sigurd. And I would say more if I weren't injured, but my wound is bleeding and coming open, and I have spoken the truth."

Now Sigurd's body was prepared in the ancient way, and a great funeral pyre was built. And when the fire had been kindled, they put Sigurd, the killer of Fáfnir, on top of it with his three-year-old son, killed on Brynhild's orders, and Guttorm. And when the fire was burning high, Brynhild spoke with her serving-women and told them to take the gold that she wanted to give them. And after this, Brynhild died and burned there with Sigurd, and their lives came to a close.

Chapter 32. The Marriage of Guđrún to King Atli

[compare *Guđrúnarkvida II (Guthrunarkvitha II)*,
st. 1–36, in the *Poetic Edda*]

Now everyone who has heard this story agrees that there will never be another man like Sigurd in the world, that no one will ever be born again who could equal him in anything, and that his name will always be famous in the German language and in Scandinavia as long as the world lasts.

It is said that one day Guđrún sat in her room and said, "My life was better when I had Sigurd. He was better than all other men, as much as gold is better than iron, or garlic is better than other plants, or a stag is better than other animals, until my brothers became jealous of this man who was better than all others, and they could not sleep until they had killed him.

"Grani neighed loudly when he saw his lord injured. And I spoke to him as I would have to a man, when he bowed his head over the earth and knew that Sigurd was fallen."

Then Guðrún went away into the woods. Everywhere she went, she heard the howling of wolves, and she thought she would be happier if she died. She wandered until she came to the hall of King Hálf, and there she stayed with Thóra, daughter of Hákon, in Denmark for three and a half years. She was made welcome there with great joy, and she made a tall tapestry, and on it she wove scenes of many great deeds and great contests which were talked about in her time, and of swords and armor and other kingly things, and the ships of King Sigmund as they departed from shore, and how Siggeir and Sigar fought on the island of Fyn.

The women found their joy in such things, and for a while Guðrún found a little comfort in her misery.

Grímhild learned where Guðrún was, and she summoned her sons, asking which one of them would go to Guðrún and offer to compensate her for the murder of her husband and son, which she said they owed her. Gunnar said that he would be happy to offer Guðrún gold to repay her for her agony, and he sent for his friends. They prepared their horses, helmets, shields, swords, and coats of chainmail and every other sort of war-gear. And this expedition was prepared in the noblest fashion, and no great champion sat at home. Their horses were given chainmail to wear, and every rider had either a gilded shield or one that had been polished until it reflected like glass. Grímhild herself went on that journey with them and said that their errand wouldn't be completed unless she went along. Altogether they were six hundred riders, and they had many excellent men with them. Valdar the Dane went with them, as did Eymóð and Jarizleif.

They went into the hall of King Hálf, where there were men of the Langobards, and of the Saxons and Franks. They went in full armor and they wore red cloaks, as the poem says:

> They had tailored shirts of chainmail,
> they had pointed helmets,
> they had swords at their belts,
> and their hair was chestnut.

They wanted to give their sister good gifts and they spoke kindly to her, but she trusted none of them. Then Grímhild gave Guđrún a cursed drink, and she was forced to accept it, and afterwards she remembered none of their crimes. This drink had been mixed with the might of the earth and the sea and the blood of Grímhild's own son, and the drinking horn itself was carved with every kind of rune and painted with blood, as it is told:

> "There were all sorts
> of runes in that horn,
> carved there and bloodied,
> I couldn't read them.
> There was a long sea serpent
> carved on the horn,
> there was an ear of wheat,
> there were animal guts.

> "Many evil things
> were mixed into that beer,
> the blood of all beasts,
> and burned acorns,
> and eagle's blood,
> and intestines, and
> boiled pig's liver, all because
> she wanted to make me forget."

And after this, when they had forced her to agree with them, there was great rejoicing.

Then Grímhild met with Guđrún and said, "Be well, my daughter. I'll bring you gold and every kind of treasure to inherit from your father, and precious rings, and bed drapings in the style the noblest Hunnish girls use, and then you'll be paid back for your husband's death. And then you will be married to the powerful King Atli and you'll have his wealth. Don't forsake your family for the sake of one man—do as we ask, instead."

Guđrún said, "I never want to marry King Atli. It would not suit us to produce children."

Grímhild said, "Don't turn your thoughts to blame. It will be as if Sigurd and Sigmund never died, if you have sons with King Atli."

Gudrún said, "I can't stop thinking about him; Sigurd was better than all other men."

Grímhild said, "You are ordered to marry this king, or you will be without a husband."

Gudrún said, "Don't offer me to this king. Only evil will come from his family, and he will do evil things to your sons and it will be avenged on him cruelly."

Grímhild was upset when Gudrún mentioned misfortune befalling her sons, and she said, "Do as I order, and you will receive great fame and my friendship, and the lands called Vínbjorg and Valbjorg." Grímhild's words were so powerful, that it had to be done.

Gudrún said, "It has to be done, though I am not willing, and this will cause more agony rather than joy."

Then the men mounted up on their horses and put the women in the wagons. They traveled seven days by land, seven days by sea, and then another seven by land, until they came to a high hall. A great crowd was there to greet her, and a wonderful feast was prepared as agreed to before, and everything was done with great honor and ceremony. And at this feast King Atli was married to Gudrún.

But her heart never smiled upon him, and their days together had little joy.

Chapter 33. Atli Sends an Invitation to the Sons of Gjúki

[compare *Gudrúnarkvitda II (Guthrunarkvitha II)*, st. 1–36, and *Atlakvida (Atlakvitha)*, st. 1–9, in the *Poetic Edda*]

Now it is told that one night King Atli woke from his sleep. He said to Gudrún, "I dreamed that you stabbed me through with a sword."

Gudrún interpreted this dream. She said that dreaming about iron was an omen of fire, "and also a sign of the arrogance of considering yourself higher than all others."

Atli said, "I went on to dream that two reeds had grown here, and I never wanted to cut them. But then they were severed from their roots and reddened in blood, and they were brought to my table and offered to me for food. Then I dreamed that two hawks flew from my hand, but they flew unluckily and they went to Hel. I dreamed that their hearts were served mixed with honey, and I ate them. Then I dreamed that two handsome puppies lay at my feet and barked, but then I ate their raw flesh against my own will."

Guðrún said, "Your dreams are not good, but these things will come to pass. Your sons are doomed, and many terrible things will happen to us."

"I dreamed further," said Atli, "that I lay in my own bed and I was killed."

Time passed, and the two said little to one another. And Atli began to wonder what had become of the great treasure that Sigurd had owned and King Gunnar and his brother Hogni now had. Atli was a great, powerful king, wise and with a large following, and he talked with his men about how to proceed. He knew that Gunnar and Hogni had much more wealth than any other men could compete with, and he decided to send messengers to seek those brothers and invite them to a feast with offers of many fine things. And the man who led these messengers was named Vingi.

Queen Guðrún noticed their secret talks and suspected that a plot was being made against her brothers. She carved a message in runes, and she took a golden ring and tied a wolf's hair around it. She gave these things to the king's messengers, who afterwards left on their mission. And before they reached Gunnar's realm, Vingi noticed the runes, and he modified them to make it seem that Guðrún had said she was eager for her brothers to come.

When the messengers came to the hall of King Gunnar, they were given a good welcome. Big fires were prepared for them, and they were given good drink to enjoy.

Vingi said, "King Atli sent me here to ask that you visit him at his home and be welcomed there and receive great honors from him, as well as helmets and shields, swords and coats of armor, gold and fine clothing, soldiers and horses and vast lands to hold as his vassal—he thinks there is no one better to leave his kingdom to than you."

Then Gunnar turned his head to Hogni and said, "How should we respond to this invitation? He's offering us great wealth, but I don't think any kings have as much gold as we do, because we have the whole treasure that was once at Gnitaheid. We have large chambers full of gold, and the best swords and all kinds of armor. I know that my horse is the best and my sword is the sharpest, and this gold the finest."

Hogni said, "I'm perplexed by his invitation, because it's something he has seldom done. I think it would be foolish to accept, and there's something else that gives me pause. In the jewels that King Atli sent us, I found a golden ring with a wolf's hair tied to it. Perhaps Gudrún thinks he has a wolf's heart toward us, and she doesn't want us to make the journey."

Then Vingi showed him the message in runes that he said Gudrún had sent.

Now most of the commoners went to sleep, but Gunnar and Hogni stayed up drinking with some men. Then Hogni's wife Kostbera, the most beautiful of women, went to look at the runes. The name of Gunnar's wife was Glaumvor, and she was a very capable and talented woman. It was the brothers' wives who were serving the drinks, and both King Gunnar and Hogni became very drunk.

Vingi did not fail to notice this, and he said, "I won't lie to you. King Atli is very old and having trouble defending his kingdom, and his sons are young and incapable. Now he means to give you his kingdom while they are still young, and he would like it best if it was you who had it."

Now, because he was very drunk, and because he was offered a great kingdom, and moreover because no one can fight fate, Gunnar promised to go to King Atli, and he told his brother Hogni.

Hogni said, "Your decision must stand, and I will follow you, though I do not go eagerly."

Chapter 34. Concerning the Dreams of Kostbera

And when the men had drunk as much as they wished, they went to sleep. Kostbera, Hogni's wife, looked at the runes and read them. She saw that something different was written underneath, and that the letters looked haphazardly written. She was wise enough to read it, though, and afterwards she went to bed with her husband.

And when they woke, she said to Hogni, "The journey you are planning away from home is unwise. Go another time, if you have to. You aren't reading clearly if you think it's your sister who invited you this time. I read her message in runes, and I was perplexed that such a wise woman would have written so poorly, but what I read underneath those runes spelled your death. I can see that she either missed a letter, or that others changed what she wrote. And now, listen to my dream. I dreamed that a river crashed into the hall, and it was very strong and it broke the pillars."

He said, "You often feel suspicious, but I don't have the personality to think badly of other men unless they prove otherwise to me. He'll greet us gladly."

She said, "You'll test that, but his friendship will not follow his invitation. And I had another dream, and in that one another river crashed into the hall and made a loud noise and broke up all the floorboards in the hall and it broke your feet and Gunnar's too, and this must mean something."

He said, "There will be fields, where you saw a river, and when we walk in the fields big barbs will often stick to our feet."

"I dreamed," she said, "that your sheets were burning and that the flames leapt high from our hall."

He said, "I know exactly what that means. Our clothes are in disorderly piles, and they will burn, even though you think you saw sheets."

"I dreamed that a bear came inside," she said, "and the bear destroyed Gunnar's throne and it struck out with its paws and we were all afraid, and then it took all of us in its mouth and we were paralyzed, and the horror was terrible."

He said, "There will be a great storm, when you dream about a polar bear."

"I dreamed that an eagle came inside," she said, "and he flew the length of the hall and drenched me and everybody else all in blood. And that must mean evil is coming, because I thought the eagle was the spirit of King Atli."

He said, "We often kill and butcher big steers for our meals, and when you dream about an eagle, it's a symbol for a steer, and Atli will be faithful to us."

And with this, their conversation ended.

Chapter 35. Gunnar and Hogni Visit Atli

[compare *Atlakvida (Atlakvitha)*, st. 10–13, in the *Poetic Edda*]

Now it is told that much the same happened when Gunnar awoke. His wife Glaumvor told him many of her dreams and said she thought it was likely that Atli would betray them. But Gunnar interpreted all of her dreams the opposite way.

"This was one of them," she said. "I dreamed that a bloody sword was brought into the hall, and you were stabbed through with it, and wolves howled on either end of the sword."

King Gunnar said, "Some small dogs will want to bite me. Barking dogs are often what dreams about bloody swords mean."

She said, "I had another dream. Some women came in, and they were sad, and they wanted to marry you. It may be that these were your family spirits."

He said, "It's not easy to interpret this dream correctly, but no one can postpone his death-day. And it's not unlikely that I have only a short time left."

And in the morning they woke up and wanted to go, though others tried to hold them back.

Then Gunnar said to a man named Fjornir, "Get up and give us good wine to drink from our big cups, because it may be that this will be our last feast and the wolf will take over our gold if we die, and the bear will fight him for it with snapping jaws."

Then the troops mustered, and the women wept. One of Hogni's sons said, "Farewell, and good luck."

They left the bigger part of their army behind. Sólar and Snævar, sons of Hogni, came with them, and so did a great champion named Orkning, brother of Hogni's wife Kostbera.

Many people followed them to their ships and tried to talk them out of the journey, but to no avail.

Then Gunnar's wife Glaumvor said, "Vingi, it is likely that bad luck will be the result of your errand. Important events await on your journey."

He answered, "I swear that I am not lying, and may a high rope hang me and demons too, if one word was a lie." And he wasn't ashamed to speak in such terms.

Kostbera said, "Farewell, and good luck."

And Hogni answered to the women, "Be cheerful, whatever happens to me."

Now husbands and wives were parted, and with them their fates. The men rowed with such strength and strain that their ship's keel was half submerged. They rowed hard with their oars so that they broke top and bottom. And when finally they came to land, they did not anchor their ships.

Now they rode their excellent horses through the dark forest a while, until they saw King Atli's home. They heard a great noise and the clashing of weapons from there, and they saw a big crowd of men and the preparations they were busy making. The whole town wall was full of men.

They rode up to the wall, and it was locked. But Hogni broke down the gate, and in they rode.

Then Vingi said, "It would be better if you hadn't done that. Wait here while I find a hanging-tree for you. I invited you here pleasantly enough, but there was deception underneath. Now it won't be long before you're both hanged!"

Hogni said, "We're not going to give in to you easily, and I don't think we're likely to be scared when the fighting starts. It's no good to try to scare us—we'll pay it all back to you ferociously."

Gunnar and Hogni kicked Vingi down, and beat him to death with their axe handles.

Chapter 36. Concerning the Battle

[compare *Atlakvida (Atlakvitha)*, st. 14–17, in the *Poetic Edda*]

Now they rode to the king's hall. King Atli had prepared his army for battle, and the troops were standing on either end of a large yard.

"Be welcome here with us," said King Atli, "and give me the golden treasure that is my proper inheritance—the money that was Sigurd's, and now belongs to Guðrún."

Gunnar said, "You'll never get that treasure, and you have good warriors to face before you'll see us dead, if you propose to fight us. It may be that you've indeed set a fine table, but that you've set it for the eagles and the wolves, and you'll be a generous host."

"I have been plotting for a long time," said Atli, "to kill the two of you, and to have all the gold for my own and pay you back for the cowardly work you did when you killed your heroic brother-in-law, and I mean to avenge him."

Hogni said, "It will be worse for you the longer you think about it. You're not ready for us."

And now a hard battle started, and to begin with it was an archer's battle. The news reached Guðrún, and when she heard about the battle, she stood up, strode forward, and threw off her cloak. She went out and greeted the guests, kissing her brothers and showing them her love, and this was their last greeting.

She said, "I thought I'd seen to it that you wouldn't come, but no one can fight fate." Then she asked: "Would it do any good to propose a peaceful settlement?"

All the men rejected this immediately. And when Guðrún saw that her brothers were the victims of foul play, her heart hardened and she put on a chainmail shirt and took up a sword and fought alongside her brothers and fought as hard as the fiercest man, and everyone agrees that there could hardly be a tougher defensive action than they fought there. There was a tremendous loss of life, and no one fought harder than Gunnar and Hogni.

The battle lasted a long time, all the way through midday. Gunnar and Hogni pushed through the ranks of King Atli's soldiers, and it is said that the valley was drowning in blood. Hogni's sons also fought their way forward hard.

Then King Atli said, "I have a big army of free men and great champions, but now many have died, and I have much to repay you for killing nineteen of my champions. I have only eleven left."

Now there was a pause in the battle. King Atli said, "I was one of four brothers, and I am the only survivor. But I married well, and I thought this would increase my fame. I had a beautiful and wise wife, fire-spirited and hard-hearted, but I could barely enjoy her wisdom because we were seldom at peace. Now you have killed many of my kinsmen, and robbed me of my kingdom and treasure, and betrayed my sister, and that is the worst of my sufferings."

Hogni said, "Why do you talk like this? You broke the peace first. You took a kinswoman of mine and murdered her by starving her to death. Then you took her wealth, and that was hardly kingly behavior. I think it's laughable to hear you airing your grievances, and I will thank the gods for whatever bad things befall you."

Chapter 37. The Death of Gunnar and Hogni

[compare *Atlakviða (Atlakvitha)*, st. 18–33, in the *Poetic Edda*]

Now King Atli urged his men forward into a forceful charge, and the fighting was fierce. Gunnar and Hogni attacked so hard that King Atli was forced back into his hall, and the fighting continued inside and became extremely violent. The battle caused huge loss of life, and it ended with the death of Gunnar and Hogni's entire army, so that the two of them were fighting alone, and many men went to Hel who were sent there by their weapons.

Now King Atli's men set upon King Gunnar, and because of their massive advantage in numbers they were able to capture him and put him in chains. Then Hogni kept fighting with great energy and reckless courage, and he killed twenty of King Atli's best champions. He shoved many of them into the fire that blazed in the middle of the hall. They all agreed that they had never before seen such a man. But in the end he was overwhelmed by their numbers and put in chains.

King Atli said, "It is a great wonder how many men Hogni has killed. Now cut out his heart and let that be his end."

Hogni said, "Do as you like. I'll await it cheerfully, whatever you decide to do, and you'll know that my heart isn't afraid. I've endured hard things before, and I was always eager to prove my manliness before I was injured. But now I have multiple wounds and you alone can decide what will happen to me."

But one of King Atli's advisors said, "I have a better plan. Let us take the slave Hjalli rather than Hogni. He's a slave made for dying, and he could never live long enough to be anything but bad anyway."

The slave heard and shouted and tried to run away to where he thought he could hide himself. He said he did not deserve this kind of rough treatment, and that he was being badly repaid for his hard work. He said it was an evil day if he was going to die and be deprived of his comfortable living and his pig farming. But they caught him and put the knife to him, and he screamed very high before he felt the knifeblade.

Then Hogni spoke up, as few men would have the courage to do in such a place. He told them to let the slave live, and said that he didn't want to hear the man's screams, and that he himself would have an easier time taking this punishment. The slave was overjoyed, and his life was spared.

Now both Gunnar and Hogni were put in chains. And King Atli told King Gunnar that he would have to tell him where the gold was if he wanted to live. Gunnar said, "First I must see the bloody heart of my brother Hogni."

Now they took the slave in hand a second time. They cut out his heart, and brought it before King Gunnar.

Gunnar said, "This is the heart of the coward Hjalli! It is nothing like my bold brother Hogni's heart, because it's trembling—and it trembled twice as much in the coward's chest."

Now on the orders of King Atli, they went again to Hogni and cut his heart out. And Hogni's manliness was so great that he laughed while he was put through this torture, and they were all amazed at his fearlessness, and it has long been remembered. They showed Hogni's heart to Gunnar.

Gunnar said, "Here you can see the heart of my bold brother Hogni! It is nothing like the coward Hjalli's heart, because it moves little now, and it moved even less in the brave man's chest. And now, Atli, you will lose your life, and I will lose mine. Now I·am the only one who knows where the gold is, and Hogni can no longer tell you. I was always in doubt while the two of us lived, but now I am certain the secret is safe with me alone. Let the river Rhine have the treasure and let the Huns never wear it."

King Atli said, "Take the prisoner away." And this was done.

Guðrún summoned her servants and then went to Atli and said, "Let your fate treat you as badly as you have treated your promises to me and Gunnar!"

King Gunnar was put into a snake-pit. There were many snakes inside, and his hands were tied together tight. Guðrún threw a harp to him, and he showed his skill and played the harp with great talent, plucking the strings with his toes. He played so well and skillfully that few thought they had heard playing as good even when they had heard the harp played with the hands. And Gunnar played so well and long that the vipers all fell asleep, except for one big, cruel snake that slithered up to him and dug in with its fangs and pierced all the way to his heart, and in this way Gunnar died while showing great courage.

Chapter 38. Guðrún's Revenge

[compare *Atlakviða (Atlakvitha)*, st. 34–45, in the *Poetic Edda*]

Now King Atli believed he had won a great victory, and he told Guðrún this mockingly and with a cruel voice. He said, "Guðrún, you have lost your brothers, and the fault is your own."

She said, "You're feeling satisfied now, when you declare these murders in my presence, but it may be that you'll regret it when you experience what's coming. The life that is left to you won't ever lose its bleakness, and things won't go well for you while I live."

He said, "We ought to make a settlement between us. I'd like to repay you for your brothers with whatever gold and precious jewels you like."

She said, "For a long time I've been hard for you to live with, although it might have been otherwise if you had let even just Hogni live.

"But now you will never be able to repay me for their lives in a way I will accept. Women are often overpowered by men's violence, and now all my kin are dead, and I have you alone to obey. I will choose this: let us have a great feast prepared, and I will do honor to the passing of my brothers and to your own kinsmen."

She spoke pleasantly, but underneath her words she was unchanged. Atli was easily persuaded, and he believed what she said when she acted as if her heart had softened. Gudrún held the funeral feast for her brothers, and King Atli for his men, and it was a lively feast.

Now Gudrún thought of her miseries and how she might inflict some great humiliation on Atli. During the evening she took her and King Atli's sons up from where they were playing by a wall. The boys were sullen and asked what they had to do.

She said, "Don't ask. You are both going to die."

They said, "You can do what you want with your own children, and no one will forbid it. But there is shame for you in doing this."

Then she cut their heads off.

The king asked later where his sons were. Gudrún said, "I'll tell you, and it will cheer your heart. You gave me untold misery when you killed my brothers. Now hear what I have to say: your sons are lost to you, and these are their skulls here for drinking cups, and you've drunk their blood mixed with wine. I took their hearts and cooked them on a spit, and you ate them."

King Atli said, "You're a cruel woman who has murdered her own sons and given me their flesh to eat. And you don't let much time pass between bad deeds."

Gudrún said, "My great wish is to hurt you awfully. I'll never be able to fully repay all the cruel deeds of such an evil king as you."

Atli said, "You've done worse things than anyone has ever heard of. It's foolish to do such hard-hearted things, and it would be proper if you were burned on a funeral pyre after being stoned to death; then you'd have what you've deserved."

She said, "You make this prophecy, but my fate is a different death." And they said many other hateful things to each other.

Hogni had a surviving son who was named Niflung. He hated Atli, and he told Gudrún that he wanted to avenge his father. She took this well and they conspired together. Gudrún told him there would be great luck in avenging his father, if he could accomplish it. And during the evening, after King Atli had been drinking, he fell asleep. Once he was sleeping, Gudrún and Niflung came, and Gudrún took up a sword and stabbed Atli in the chest. This was the plan she had made with Niflung.

King Atli woke up when he felt the strike and said, "There won't be any need to bandage or doctor this injury, but who are you who killed me?"

Gudrún said, "The blame is partly on me, and partly on Hogni's son."

Atli said, "This was not an honorable deed, even if there was some cause for it. You were married to me with your family's blessing, and I paid the price they set for you, thirty good knights and good young women, and many other followers besides. But you could not abide it unless you controlled all the lands that belonged to my father King Budli, and you have often left your mother-in-law in tears."

Gudrún said, "You've told lie after lie. I don't care. I was often hard to get along with, and you made it worse. There has often been strife in your home, and your kinsmen and friends have often fought one another, and each started feuds with another.

"My life was better when I was with Sigurd. We would kill kings and take their wealth. And we gave peace to those who wanted it, and great chieftains came and submitted to us and we let them keep their realms if they wished. But then I lost him. I could have endured staying a widow, but not being married to you, a man who has never been on the better side of any battle, not when I had been married to the best king."

King Atli said, "That is not true, but this argument won't make you or me happier, and I am already defeated. Now do me some honor, and let my funeral be prepared nobly."

She said, "I will let you have an honorable burial, and I will order a worthy stone coffin built for you. I will weave handsome cloths to wrap your body in, and I will attend to every other need."

After this he died, and Gudrún did as she had promised. And afterwards she burned his hall down, and when his handpicked men woke up in the hour before dawn, they did not want to burn, and they killed each other with their weapons instead. And in this way the life of King Atli, and every one of his best men, was ended. Gudrún did not wish to live after this, but her death-day had not yet come. And now the hostilities ended in this way, for a while.

It is said that the Volsungs and the children of Gjúki were the proudest and noblest people who have been told of in the ancient poems.

Chapter 39. The Marriage of King Jónakr to Guđrún

[compare the prose introduction to *Guđrúnarhvot*
(Guthrunarhvot) in the *Poetic Edda*]

Guđrún had a daughter with Sigurđ named Svanhild. She was the most beautiful of all women, and she had fierce eyes like her father's, so that few dared to look her in the eye. She was more beautiful than other women, just as the sun is brighter than all other lights in the sky.

Guđrún went to the sea one day and put her arms around a large stone and then threw herself to the ocean. She wanted to die. But the waves took her up, and she floated to the town of King Jónakr. He was a powerful king with a large following. He married Guđrún, and they had three sons: Hamdir, Sorli, and Erp. Svanhild was brought up there as well.

Chapter 40. Concerning Jormunrekk and Svanhild

[compare the prose introduction to *Guđrúnarhvot*
(Guthrunarhvot) in the *Poetic Edda*]

A king was named Jormunrekk, a very powerful king in his time. His son was named Randvér. The king came to talk with his son and said, "You will go on an errand for me to King Jónakr, together with my counselor Bikki. There is a girl named Svanhild in King Jónakr's land. She is the daughter of Sigurđ, killer of Fáfnir, and she is the most beautiful woman under the sun. I want her in preference to anyone else, and you are going to propose that she be married to me."

Randvér said, "It is my duty, my lord, to go on your errand." He had the expedition prepared splendidly, and they traveled until they came to King Jónakr's home where they saw Svanhild, and they thought that her beauty was remarkable.

Randvér sought an audience with King Jónakr and said, "King Jormunrekk wants to propose marriage to your stepdaughter. He has heard of Svanhild and he wants her for his wife, and it would be impossible to marry her to a more powerful man than he is."

The king said that this was a good idea, and that Jormunrekk was very famous.

Gudrún said, "It's foolish to trust that a streak of good luck won't break."

But with the encouragement of King Jormunrekk, and because of every argument that was brought to bear in favor of the marriage, it was agreed, and Svanhild went to Randvér's ship with a worthy following and sat in the stern with Randvér.

Then Bikki said to Randvér, "It would be more fitting for you, and not the old man, to have such a beautiful woman." This agreed well with Randvér's feelings, and he went and spoke to her pleasantly, and she to him.

Later they came home and met the king.

Bikki said, "It is fitting, lord, for you to know what has happened, though it is painful to say it. The news is that you have been betrayed, and your son has enjoyed Svanhild's love in every way. She is his concubine, and you should not let such things go unpunished."

Bikki had often given evil counsel before, though this did worse evil than anything else he had ever done. The king listened to his many evil words, and then he said, while he was unable to control himself in his rage, that Randvér should be taken and hanged. And when Randvér had been led to the hanging-tree, he took a hawk in his hand and plucked off all its feathers and said that it ought to be shown to his father.

And when the king saw this, he said, "Now I see that he thinks I've been stripped of honor, like this hawk has been stripped of feathers." And he ordered him taken down from the hanging-tree. But Bikki had done his deceitful work, and Jormunrekk's son was already dead. Now Bikki said, "You have no one to repay worse than Svanhild. Let her die with shame."

King Jormunrekk said, "That is advice I will take." And she was tied up by the town gate and horses were let loose to trample her. But when she stared at the horses, they didn't dare come near her. Bikki saw this and said that a bag should be put over her head, and this was done, and then she was killed.

Chapter 41. Guðrún Urges Her Sons to Take Vengeance

[compare *Guðrúnarhvot (Guthrunarhvot)* and *Hamðismál (Hamthismal)*, st. 1–10, in the *Poetic Edda*]

Guðrún learned about the death of Svanhild and told her sons, "Why do you sit here so quietly, speaking pleasantly, when Jormunrekk has killed your sister and trampled her under horses' hooves with shame? You two have hearts nothing like Gunnar and Hogni's. They would have avenged their kinswoman."

Hamðir said, "You didn't have much good to say about Gunnar and Hogni when they killed Sigurð and made you red with his blood. And you avenged your brothers evilly when you killed your own sons, and it would be better if all of us were alive to go and kill King Jormunrekk together. But we won't stand idly by for these mocking words, not when you push us so hard."

Guðrún laughed and gave them big cups to drink from. And afterwards she chose massive, well-made shirts of chainmail for them to wear, and other clothes of war.

Then Hamðir said, "This will be our last parting, and you'll hear the news of it. You'll drink the funeral toast for Svanhild, and for the two of us too." And then they left.

Guðrún went to her room more miserable than ever and said, "I was married to three men, first to Sigurð, killer of Fáfnir. He was betrayed, and that was my greatest misery.

"Then I was married to King Atli, and my heart hated him so much that I killed my own sons in my grief.

"Then I went to the sea, and the waves threw me back on land and I was given to this king. Then I married Svanhild off with great wealth, and the worst of my miseries after Sigurð's death is that she was trampled under the hooves of horses. But the cruelest of my miseries is that Gunnar was thrown in the snake-pit, and the hardest is that Hogni's heart was cut out.

"It would be better if Sigurð would come to me and I could go away with him. Now I sit with no sons or daughters to comfort me.

"Sigurð, do you remember what we said, when we first stepped together into one bed—that either you would come back to me from Hel, or wait for me there?"

And this was the last of what Guðrún had to say about her torments.

Chapter 42. The Murder of Erp and the Fall of Sorli and Hamdir

[compare *Hamðismál (Hamthismal)*, st. 11–31, in the *Poetic Edda*]

Now it is told that Guðrún had enchanted the armor of her sons so that iron could not pierce it, and she told them not to injure any stones or other big things and that if they did, they would no longer be shielded from all harm.

And when they had started on their way, they met their brother Erp, and they asked him what help he would give them.

He said, "I will help you like hand helps hand, or foot helps foot."

They thought he meant no help at all, and they killed him. Then they rode along further, and a little later Hamdir tripped and caught himself with his hand and said, "Erp must have been speaking faithfully. I would have fallen just now if I hadn't caught myself with my hand."

And a little later Sorli also tripped. He recovered himself with his foot, and steadied himself. He said, "I would have fallen, if I hadn't caught myself with both feet." Now they said that they had done an evil thing to their brother Erp.

They went on to the realm of King Jormunrekk, and they went before him and attacked him. Hamdir cut off both his hands, and Sorli both his feet.

Then Hamdir said, "His head would have come off, too, if our brother Erp had lived, but we killed him on the road and we realized our error too late," as the poem says:

> "Jormunrekk would lose his head,
> if only Erp still lived,
> our bold brother,
> the one we killed on the road."

And when they had done this, they had violated the command of their mother, because they had injured stone. Now Jormunrekk's men attacked them, and they defended themselves well and boldly and injured many men, and iron would not harm them.

But then an old man came, very tall and with only one eye, and he said, "You are not wise if you don't know how to kill these men."

King Jormunrekk said, "Advise us if you know how."

The man said, "Kill them with stones."

And this was done. Stones were thrown at them from every direction, and they were killed.

The Saga of Ragnar Loðbrók
(*Ragnars saga loðbrókar*)

Chapter 1. Concerning Heimir and Áslaug

Now the news came to Heimir in Hlymdalir that Sigurð and Brynhild were dead. Their daughter Áslaug, who was Heimir's foster-daughter, was three years old at the time, and Heimir knew that someone would search for her and try to kill her and wipe out her family line. And he mourned so much for the loss of Brynhild, his foster-daughter, that he could not hold on to his kingdom or his wealth, and he knew that he could not hide the girl there. So he had a huge harp made, and he hid Áslaug inside of it together with many treasures of gold and silver, and then he wandered north through many lands until he came here to Scandinavia.

This harp was so skillfully made that he could take it apart and put it back together in sections. During the days when he walked near the wild waterfalls and was far from any farm, Heimir would take the harp apart and wash the girl. And he had a particular onion that he would give her to eat, and this onion had the power that a person could eat it and live, even if no other food was available. And when the girl cried, he would play the harp and then she would be quiet, because Heimir was skillful at all the arts that were popular in his time. He also kept many precious clothes in the harp with the girl, together with a great deal of gold.

And now Heimir traveled until he came to Norway and entered a little farm there that was called Spangarheið. The man who lived there was named Aki, and his wife was named Gríma, and there were no other people besides them there.

On the day Heimir arrived, the husband had gone into the forest, but the old woman was at home. She greeted Heimir and asked what sort of man he might be. He said he was a beggar, and he asked the old woman to let him stay the night. She said not very many guests visited, but that she would be hospitable to him, if he thought he needed to stay there. And Heimir said the best hospitality he could hope for on his journey would be if a fire could be started for him, and then if he could be led to the sleeping quarters where he could spend the night.

And when the old woman had gotten a fire started, Heimir stood the harp up next to where he sat. The woman spoke constantly, and her glance often turned toward the harp, because it happened that a piece of precious cloth hung out from inside it. And as Heimir was warming himself up at the fire, she saw a precious golden ring that appeared from underneath his tattered clothes, because he was poorly dressed. And when he had warmed himself and was comfortable, he ate dinner. And after this he asked the old woman to show him to the place where he could sleep for the night.

Then the old woman said that it would be better for him to sleep outside than inside, "Because I'm often talkative with my husband when he comes home."

Heimir said it was her decision to make, so he went outside with her. He took the harp and kept it with him. The old woman went out and led him to where there was a barn and said that he could situate himself there and that she thought he could enjoy a night's sleep there. And now the old woman left and did the chores she needed to do, and Heimir went to sleep.

Aki came home as the evening drew on, and found that his wife had done few of the chores she was supposed to do. He was angry when he came home and he spoke to her roughly, because everything that he had told her to do was undone. He said that there was a lot of difference between how much he and she enjoyed their day, because he had to work more than he could every day, but she wouldn't do anything useful.

"Don't be angry, husband," she said, "because maybe in a short time you'll be able to do something that will make us happy for the rest of our lives."

"What is that?" he asked.

She said, "A man has come here to our home, and I think he's traveling with a great deal of money, and he's getting old. He probably once was a great champion, but now he is very tired. I don't think I've ever seen his equal, but I think he's worn out and sleeping."

Then Aki said, "I don't think it's wise to betray the few people who ever come here."

Gríma said, "You will always be a man of little ambition, because everything seems to be a bigger thing in your eyes than it is. Well, either you will kill him, or I will marry him and then he and I will kick you out of here. And I can tell you what he said to me last night, although you won't think well of it. He spoke seductively to me, and I think I'd like to have him for a husband and drive you off or kill you, if you don't want to do what I want."

And it is told that Aki was easily dominated by his wife, and she kept up her nagging until he gave in, and he took up his axe and sharpened it well. And when he was ready, the woman followed Aki to where Heimir was sleeping, and he was snoring loudly.

Then Gríma told Aki that he should attack him as hard as he could, "and then run away quickly, because I doubt you can stand his shouting and screaming if he gets his hands on you." Then she grabbed the harp and ran away with it, and he stepped up to the spot where Heimir slept. He hit him hard with the axe, and it was a big wound and the axe flew out of his hands. Then he ran away as fast as he could.

Heimir woke up when he was attacked, and he felt that it was his death-blow. And it is said that he made such a loud noise in his final agony that the pillars of the building collapsed and then the whole building with them, and there was a great earthquake, and in this way his life came to an end.

Now Aki came to where Gríma was and told her that he had killed Heimir. "But there was a while when I wasn't sure how it would go, because he was a very great man. But I think he is now in Hel."

Gríma said that he deserved thanks for doing this. "And I think we have plenty of money now, and we'll test whether what I said is true." So they started a fire, and Gríma took the harp and wanted to take it apart, but she knew no other way than to break it because she did not have Heimir's skill. She broke it open, and she saw a very young girl inside of a sort she thought she had never seen, and there was also a large amount of treasure inside the harp with her.

Aki said, "Now it's happened like it often does, that one is punished for betraying those who trust him. It looks like we have another mouth to feed on our hands."

Gríma said, "This is not what I expected, but it's not a bad surprise." She asked the girl what family she was from, but the girl said nothing, as if she had never learned to speak.

"Now it's going as I expected, that our evil deed has brought us evil," said Aki. "We have committed a terrible crime, and what are we going to do with this child?"

"That's simple," said Gríma. "She'll be named Kráka ['Crow'], after my mother."

Aki said again, "What are we going to do with her?"

Gríma said, "I have a good idea. We'll say she's our daughter and we'll raise her."

"No one will believe it," said Aki. "This child is much better-looking than we are, and we are both incredibly ugly. No one will think it's believable that we had a child who looks like this, considering how hideous we both are."

Gríma said, "You don't understand, but I have an idea for how to make it more believable. I'll shave her bald and then put tar and other things in her scalp to keep her hair from growing back. And she'll wear a long hood, and she'll never wear good clothes. Then our looks won't seem so different, and maybe people will think that I was much better-looking in my youth. Plus, she'll do all the worst work."

Gríma and Aki thought the girl could not speak, since she never answered them. And they followed Gríma's plan, and the girl grew up with them in abject poverty.

Chapter 2. Concerning Thóra Town-Doe

Herrud was the name of a great and powerful jarl in Götaland. He was married, and his daughter was named Thóra. She was the most beautiful of all women to look at, and she was the noblest in every woman's skill that might come up or that it might be better to be with than without. The nickname she was called by was Town-Doe, because she exceeded other women in beauty just as the doe exceeds all other animals. The jarl loved his daughter dearly, and he made a little house for her near the king's hall, with a fence around it. It was the jarl's custom to send his daughter something to play with every day, and he said that he intended to continue doing so.

It is told that one day he had a small snake brought to her that was very pretty. She liked the snake and let it sit in a small chest and she put gold underneath it. It did not sit there long before it began to grow, and the gold grew that was under it. Finally there was no more room for it in the chest and the snake lay coiled in a ring around it. And later there wasn't even enough space for it in Thóra's cabin, and the snake kept growing and so did the gold. Now it lay outside and encircled the cabin so that its head touched its tail, and it did not like to be approached, and no one dared to come near the cabin because of this dragon, except the man assigned to feed it, and the dragon required a whole steer for every meal.

The jarl thought this dragon was a curse, and he swore that he would marry his daughter to whatever man could kill it, no matter what family he was from, and also give him the gold that lay beneath the dragon as a wedding-gift. This news was spread widely around the land, although no one dared to kill the great dragon.

Chapter 3. Ragnar Kills the Dragon

At that time Sigurð Ring ruled Denmark. He was a powerful king and had become famous after his battle against Harald Wartooth on Brávellir when he killed Harald, which has become known to everyone in the northern half of the world.

Sigurð Ring had a son named Ragnar. He was a big man, handsome and well-provided with wisdom. He was good to his men and cruel to his enemies. As soon as he had grown old enough, he assembled an army and a fleet of ships and became the best kind of warrior, so that there were few who could equal him.

Ragnar heard tell of what Jarl Herruð had said, but he paid it no attention and acted as if he had never heard it. But he ordered some clothes made for himself of a strange type, shaggy pants and a shaggy cloak, and when they were done, he ordered them boiled in pitch, and then he put them away.

One summer, when Ragnar sailed with his army to Götaland, he hid his ship in an inconspicuous spot in a fjord not far from where Jarl Herrud ruled. And when Ragnar had been there one night, he woke up early in the morning, rose up, and put on the same clothes as have been previously described. He took up a great spear in his hand and left the ships on his own, and he went down to a sandy place and he rolled around in the sand. And before he continued, he took the nail out of his spear that held the shaft to the point, and now he went alone from his ships to the jarl's residence and came early in the day, when everyone was sleeping.

Now Ragnar turned toward Thóra's cabin, and when he came inside the fence where the dragon was, he stabbed his spear into the dragon and pulled the spear back, and then he stabbed at the dragon again. The spear pierced the dragon's back, and then Ragnar twisted the spear so swiftly that the spearhead came loose from the shaft. The dragon made so much noise as it died that the cabin shook all around.

Now Ragnar went away. A splash of the dragon's blood hit him between the shoulders, but it did not harm him because the clothes he had made protected him.

The people inside the cabin awoke from the noise and went outside. Thóra saw a big man walking away and asked his name and where he was going. He stopped and spoke this poem:

> "Beautiful woman,
> I have honorably risked
> my life, fifteen years old,
>   to fight the serpent.
> I would be dead
> from the snake's bite
> if my spear had not bitten
> the viper's heart sooner."

Now he went away and said nothing more to her. But his spearpoint remained in the dragon's wound, though Ragnar took his spearshaft with him.

When Thóra heard his poem, she understood what he said about what he'd done, and how old he was. She thought about who he might be, but she did not know whether he was even human or not, because it seemed to her that his size, for someone of his age, was like that of a monster. She returned to her room and went back to sleep.

And when people came outside later in the morning, they saw that the dragon was dead, wounded by the big spearpoint that was still in the wound. The jarl ordered the spearpoint taken out, and it was so large that it could not have served many men as a useful weapon. Now the jarl thought about what he had said about the man who managed to kill the dragon, though he did not know whether this had been accomplished by a human man or not. He spoke with his friends and his daughter about how he should look for the man, and he thought it likely that this man would want the reward that had been promised.

Thóra suggested that a great meeting should be called, "And declare this: that all men should come who are able and who don't want to face the jarl's anger. And if the man who killed the dragon is one of them, he will probably have with him the spearshaft that fits the spearpoint."

The jarl thought this was a good idea, and he called together a meeting. And when the day came for the meeting, the jarl and many other chieftains came, and there was a great crowd.

Chapter 4. Ragnar Marries Thóra

It was heard on Ragnar's ships that the meeting was a short time away, and Ragnar went to the meeting with nearly all his men. And when they arrived, they stood a certain distance from the other men, because Ragnar saw that a great crowd had come, as was expected.

Then the jarl stood up and commanded silence and spoke. He said his thanks to the men who had carried out his orders so well, and then he told of what had taken place. First he told them what he had promised as a reward for the man who killed the dragon, and then, "The dragon is now dead, and the man who did this great deed left his spearpoint in the wound. And if the man who has the matching spearshaft is one of you here at this meeting, let him bring it forward and prove the story. Then I will do everything that I have promised, whether he is of low or high birth." And he concluded his speech by ordering that the spearhead be taken around to every man at the meeting, and ordering his men to ask each man present who owned it or who had the spearshaft that it matched. This was done, but the man who had the spearshaft was not found.

Yet when the jarl's men came to where Ragnar was standing, and showed him the spearhead, he admitted that it was his, and the spearshaft and spearhead matched. Now the men thought it was certain that it was he who had killed the dragon, and because of this deed he became very famous throughout Scandinavia, and he asked for the hand of Thóra, the jarl's daughter, and the jarl took this well. And now she was promised to Ragnar, and a great feast was prepared with all the best delicacies in that kingdom, and the wedding took place at this feast.

And when the feast was finished, Ragnar went home to his own kingdom and ruled it, and he loved Thóra well. They had two sons: the older was named Eirek, and the younger Agnar, and both were big and handsome and much stronger than most other men who were alive at the time. They learned all kinds of skills.

And one day Thóra became ill, and she died of her sickness. Ragnar took this so badly that he did not want to rule any longer. He set up other men to rule in his stead along with his sons. And at this time Ragnar took up the same practice he had followed earlier, and went raiding. And wherever he went, he took the victory.

Chapter 5. Concerning Ragnar and Kráka

Now one summer, Ragnar sailed to Norway because he had many kinsmen and friends there and he wanted to see them. One evening in Norway he came to a little harbor and he rested his ships there for the night. There was a farm a short distance away which was called Spangarheid.

When morning came, his servants were supposed to go to land to bake bread. They saw that there was a farm just a short distance away, and they thought it would be better to go to the house and do their task there. And when they came to the little farm, they found one person there, and it was an old woman, and they asked her whether she was the lady of the house and what her name was.

She answered that she was the lady of the house, "And my name is unusual. I am named Gríma. But who are you?"

They said they were servants of Ragnar Loðbrók, and they wanted to do their chores, "And we would like it if you helped us work."

The old woman answered that her hands were very stiff. "Although once it was said that I could do my chores very well. But I have a daughter who might work with you, and she will be home soon. Her name is Kráka. It's gotten to where I can barely tell her what to do."

On this morning Kráka was seeing to the livestock when she saw that many large ships had come to land, and she went and washed herself. Gríma had forbidden her to do this, because she did not want anyone to see her beauty since she was the most gorgeous of all women, and her hair was so long that it fell to the earth around her and was as beautiful as the loveliest silk.

Now Kráka came home, and Ragnar's servants had made a fire. Kráka saw that men who were unknown to her had arrived. She looked at them, and they at her.

The servants asked Gríma, "Is this your daughter? This beautiful woman?"

"It is no lie," said Gríma, "She is my daughter."

"You two are extremely different," said the men, "considering how ugly you are. And we have never seen such a beautiful woman. She seems not to have taken after you at all, since you're the worst kind of misshapen thing."

Gríma said, "Don't judge me by my looks now. My beauty is nothing like what it used to be."

Now the men said that Kráka ought to help them work. She asked, "What kind of work should I do?"

They said that they wanted her to make loaves of bread that they would bake. And she took up this work, and did it well. And they watched her the whole time, so that they neglected their own chores and burned the bread.

And when they were done with their work, they went back to the ships. And when the breakfast was served, everyone said that the servants had never done such a bad job and that they deserved to be punished for it.

Ragnar asked them why they had prepared the food so badly, and they said that they had seen a woman so beautiful that they couldn't pay attention to their chores, and they thought there couldn't be a woman more beautiful than she was in the entire world. And since they spoke so emphatically about this woman's beauty, Ragnar said she could not be as beautiful as Thóra had been, and he knew that for a fact. But his servants said she was definitely not any less beautiful.

Then Ragnar said, "I will send some men who I know have good eyesight. And if it is as you say, then your negligence will be forgiven. But if the woman is less beautiful than you say in any respect, you will be punished severely." And now he sent his men to find this beautiful woman, but there was such a strong wind against them that they could not travel that day, and so Ragnar said to his messengers, "If you think this young woman is as beautiful as I have been told, tell her to come visit me. Tell her I want to meet her and I want her to be mine. But I don't want her to be clothed or naked, fed or starving, and I don't want her to come alone, though I want no other person to come with her."

Now the messengers went back to the house. They looked as much as they needed at Kráka, and the woman seemed so beautiful to them that they thought they had never seen another so beautiful. And they passed along the words of their master Ragnar about how she should come to him.

Kráka thought about how the king had said she should come to him, but Gríma thought it was impossible to do and that the king couldn't possibly be sane. But Kráka said, "Since he said it, it must be possible to do, if I just understand what he means. I certainly can't come today, but I will come early tomorrow morning to your ships."

Now the messengers left, and told Ragnar they had done as he asked, and that she would come to meet him.

Kráka stayed at home that night, and early in the morning she told the farmer Aki that she was going to see Ragnar. "But I will need to change my clothing somewhat. You have a fishing net that I will wrap around myself, and I will let my hair fall around it, and then I will not be naked. And I will chew on one onion, and that is only a little food, but just the same it can be said that I ate. And I will have your dog follow me, so that I won't be alone, but no person will be with me."

When Gríma heard her plan, she thought the girl was wise. And when Kráka was ready, she walked to the ships. She was a beautiful sight, and her hair was so bright that to look at it was like looking at gold. And now Ragnar called to her and asked her who she was and whether there was someone she wished to meet with there. She answered with this poem:

> "I did not dare to break your order,
> when you told me to come,
> I did not dare to disobey
> what Ragnar commanded.
> No person is with me,
> and my skin is not bare,
> though I am not alone
> and I am not clothed."

Now Ragnar sent men to meet her and bring her onto his ships. But Kráka said she did not want to go unless she and the dog were both greeted with peaceful intent. Then she was led onto the king's ship, and when she came to his place on the deck, the king bowed to her, and her dog bit his hand. His men leapt forward to kill the dog, garroting the dog's throat with a bowstring and killing it that way. They did not hold the peace with her any better than this.

Ragnar laid her down in his quarters next to him and spoke to her, and she pleased him greatly and he was cheerful with her. He spoke this poem:

> "If the lovely lady
> likes this warrior,
> she will certainly
> take his hand."

She said:

> "My lord, I have
> come only to visit you.
> If you will honor our pact,
> let me go home."

Chapter 6. Ragnar Weds Kráka

Ragnar told Kráka that he desired her, and that he wanted her to come with him. She said this was impossible. Then he said that he wanted her to stay the night on his ship.

She said this would not happen before he had come back from the trip he planned, "And it may be that you will feel differently afterwards."

Then Ragnar called to his treasurer and commanded him to find a shirt that Thóra had owned, which was sewn all with gold, and bring it to him. Then he offered it to Kráka in this way:

> "Will you receive this,
> which was owned by Thóra,
> this shirt worked in silver?
> It suits you very well.
> Her beautiful hands
> touched these treasures;
> I loved that woman
> till death parted us."

Kráka said in response:

> "I don't dare to take it,
> the treasure of Queen Thóra,
> a shirt worked in silver.
> Ugly clothes are what suit me.
> I am called Kráka, 'Crow,'
> in my coal-black clothes,
> and I walk in the scree
> and herd my poor goats."

She continued, "I will certainly not accept this shirt. I'm not going to dress like a queen while I live among peasants. Maybe you'd like me better if I were dressed better, but I want to go home now. You can send men for me later if you still feel the same and want me to come with you."

Ragnar told her that he would not change his mind.

Now Kráka went home, and once they had a favorable wind, Ragnar and his men sailed on as they had originally planned, and he did everything he intended there. And when he came back the second time, he sailed into the same harbor where he had anchored before when Kráka had come to him. And that night he sent messengers to find her and tell her that Ragnar said she should come with him for good. But Kráka replied that she would not leave before the morning.

Kráka woke up early in the morning and went to the bed of Aki and Gríma and asked if they were sleeping. They said they were awake and asked what she wanted. She said that she intended to go away and not stay there any longer. "But I know that you two killed Heimir, my foster-father, and there is no one I owe worse than you. Still I will not have anything cruel done to you, because I have been with you a long time.

"But I will say this: Each day will be worse for you than the last, and your final day will be your worst. And now we part forever."

Then she went to the ships, and she was welcomed well, and the winds were favorable. That evening, when the men went to bed, Ragnar said he wanted Kráka to sleep in the same bed with him.

She said this would not happen, "And I want you to marry me, when we get back to your kingdom. I think that I am worth that, as are you and our children, if we have any."

He honored her request, and the journey went well for them. Then they returned to Ragnar's kingdom, and a great feast was prepared to greet him, and they drank ale in celebration of him and his marriage.

And the first evening when they shared the same bed, Ragnar wanted to make love to his wife. But she asked to be excused from this, and told him he would be punished for it if she didn't get her way. Ragnar said he didn't believe it, and he said neither one of them was an old man or woman with second sight. He asked how long this would go on. She said:

> "We will live in the hall
> three nights together,
> then we'll pray to the gods
> and make a sacrifice.
> Otherwise there will be

a curse on the son I bear:
if you are too eager to have me,
he will be born with no bones."

And though she recited this poem, Ragnar ignored it, and he did as he desired.

Chapter 7. Concerning the Sons of Ragnar

Time passed, and their life together was good, with much love. Then Kráka became pregnant and in due time she gave birth to a boy. The boy was sprinkled with water and given the name of Ívar. But the boy was boneless, and it felt as though there was only gristle where the bones would be. And while he was still young, his height was such that there were few men as tall as he was. He was the handsomest of all men, and so wise that it is unlikely there was ever a wiser man than he was.

Ragnar and Kráka had still more children. Their second was named Bjorn, the third Hvítserk, and the fourth Rognvald. They were all great men and the boldest of warriors, and as soon as they were old enough they learned all sorts of skills. And wherever they went, Ívar had himself carried on a stretcher because he could not walk, and he was the brothers' leader in whatever they attempted.

Now Eirek and Agnar, sons of Ragnar and Thóra, were also great men, such that one could hardly find their equal, and they went out on warships every summer and they became prominent men because of their raids.

And now one day Ívar spoke to his brothers Hvítserk and Bjorn and asked them how long they would go on with sitting around at home and not seeking out their fame. And they said that he would have the deciding vote about that, as he did about everything else.

Ívar said, "I want us to ask for ships, and for troops so that they'll be well-manned, and then I think we should go and get ourselves treasure and fame, if there's any out there to get." And when they agreed to this, they went to Ragnar and told him they wanted ships, and men to man them who were experienced in battle and ready for anything.

Ragnar gave them what they asked for, and they sailed away when the troops were ready. And wherever they fought against other men, they had the upper hand, and they won more followers and more treasure. And now Ívar said to the others that he wanted to go where they would find more opposition, and where they could really test their manliness. They asked where he thought this might be.

Ívar mentioned a place that was called Hvítabø, where sacrifices had been held, "And many have tried to conquer it, and none have succeeded. Ragnar himself went there and was forced back without taking it."

"Is there a large army there," asked the others, "one very difficult to beat, or are there other obstacles?"

Ívar said that it was both very densely populated and a great place of sacrifices, and this had stopped everyone who had come and none of them had managed to take it.

They said that Ívar would decide whether they ought to go there or not. And Ívar said that he would rather risk their courage and see if it was more powerful than the sacrifices of the people of Hvítabø.

Chapter 8. The Ragnarssons Conquer Hvítabø

Now they sailed for Hvítabø, and when they made landfall there, they prepared themselves for the assault. They thought that some of the troops ought to guard the ships, and it seemed to them that their brother Rognvald was too young to be a capable fighter in such a great test of men as this battle was likely to be, so they had him guard the ships together with some of the troops.

Before they departed their ships, Ívar told the troops that the town's inhabitants had two young steers, and that men had run away from them on account of being unable to endure their terrible noises and magic. Then Ívar said, "Stand against them as best you can, even if they frighten you—and you will not be thought less of, if so."

Now they assembled their army, and when they came near the city, the inhabitants noticed them and let loose these steers that they believed in. And when the steers were set loose, they ran forward hard and made terrible noises. Ívar saw this from where he was being carried on a shield, and he asked for his bow, and it was given to him. He then shot these evil steers, killing both of them, and in this way they were done with the obstacle that men found most frightening.

Rognvald spoke to the men on the ships and said that men were lucky if they had as much fun as his brothers were having. "And they had no other plan than to make me stay here so they would get all the honor. But now we will go out there and join them."

They did so, and when they came to where the troops were fighting, Rognvald pushed hard into the battle, and it came about that he was killed. And at this time his brothers entered the city walls and the battle began anew, and it ended with the people of Hvítabø fleeing and the sons of Ragnar chasing after them.

And when they returned to the city, Bjorn spoke this poem:

> "We raised a great war-cry,
> and I tell you the truth:
> our swords bit harder
> than theirs in Gnípafjord.
> Each man who wished to,
> became a killer outside Hvítabø;
> the boys weren't stingy
> with sword-blows."

And when they returned to the city, they took all the money and movable property, and they burned every house and broke down all the walls. And then they sailed away.

Chapter 9. Áslaug's Ancestry Comes to Light

Eystein was the name of the king who ruled Sweden at this time. He was married, and his daughter was named Ingibjorg. She was the most beautiful of all women, the best of all to look upon. King Eystein was powerful and popular, cruel and yet wise. His throne was at Uppsala. He was a great maker of sacrifices, and in his time at Uppsala there were such huge sacrifices that there were never greater ones anywhere in Scandinavia.

The Swedes had a superstition about a cow they called Síbilja. So many sacrifices had been made to this cow that no one could withstand hearing the terrible sounds it made. And it was the king's custom, when he expected war, to let this cow lead his troops, and so much demonic power was in this cow that Eystein's enemies, when they heard it, were driven so crazy that they fought among themselves and did not heed their own friends. And for this reason the Swedes were left in peace, because no man dared to fight against such overwhelming power.

King Eystein was a good friend to many men and chieftains, and it is said there was great friendship between King Eystein and Ragnar at this time. They had the custom of visiting each other for a feast in alternating summers.

It came time for Ragnar to visit Eystein for a feast. When he arrived in Uppsala, he and his men were welcomed well. After they had drunk the first evening, King Eystein ordered his daughter to serve Ragnar and himself. Ragnar's men spoke among themselves, saying that there was nothing for Ragnar to do except to ask for the hand of the king's daughter and no longer be married to a farmer's daughter. Each of his men encouraged him to do this, and it ended with Eystein's daughter engaged to Ragnar, though she was not to be married to him for some time.

When the feast ended, Ragnar went home, and his journey was without incident. Nothing is said of his travels until he was a short way from his home and his path led him through a certain forest. He and his men came to a clearing in the woods, and then Ragnar ordered his men to halt. Then he told them to listen, and he told all his men who had been with him on his visit to the Swedes that they were forbidden to talk about his plan to marry the daughter of King Eystein. He added, by way of emphasis, that if anyone did speak of it, he would lose nothing less than his life.

When he had said what he wanted, he went home. His men were happy when he returned home, and they drank beer in celebration of his return.

When he sat down once again on his throne and had not been there very long, Kráka came into the hall and sat on Ragnar's lap. She placed her arms around his neck and asked, "What is the news?"

Ragnar said there was nothing to tell. As the evening passed, the men drank and went to sleep.

When Ragnar and Kráka went to bed, she asked him again what the news was, and he said he didn't know any. She wanted to keep talking, but Ragnar said he was very sleepy and worn out from traveling.

"Then I will tell you some news," she said. "If you won't tell me any." He asked what this news might be.

"I call it news," she said, "if a king is engaged to a woman, when some would say that he already has a wife."

"Who told you this?" asked Ragnar.

"Let your men keep their lives and limbs, because none of them told me," she said. "You must have seen that three birds sat in the tree nearby you, and it was they who told me this news. I ask you not to do this thing you have planned, and I tell you that I am a king's daughter, not a farmer's, and my father was such a great man that there has never been his equal, and my mother was the wisest and most beautiful of all women, and her name will be famous as long as the world lasts."

Ragnar asked who her father was, if she was not the daughter of the poor farmer at Spangarheid. She said that she was the daughter of Sigurd, killer of Fáfnir, and that her mother was Brynhild, daughter of Budli.

Ragnar said, "It seems extremely unlikely to me that their daughter would be named 'Crow' or that their child would grow up in such poverty as I saw at Spangarheid."

Then she said, "There is a story behind this." And she told him, beginning her story with Sigurd's meeting with Brynhild on the mountain, where she was conceived. "And when Brynhild gave birth, I was given the name Áslaug." And now she told him everything that had happened since she and Heimir first met Aki and Gríma.

"These are terrible things that you say happened to Áslaug," said Ragnar.

She said, "You know that I am pregnant. The child I give birth to will be a boy, and that boy will have an odd trait: it will seem that a snake is in the boy's eye. And if this comes true, I ask that you not return to the Swedes at the time you agreed to marry King Eystein's daughter. But if this does not come true, then do as you want. But I want the boy to be named after my father if this mark of distinction is in his eye, as I predict it will be."

The time came when Áslaug felt the birth-pangs coming, and then she gave birth and the child was a boy. The midwives took the boy and showed her. Then she said that he should be taken to Ragnar for him to see. This was done, and the young boy was brought into the hall and laid on Ragnar's lap. When Ragnar saw the boy, they asked him what he should be named. He spoke this poem:

> "His name will be Sigurd,
> this boy will make battles;
> they will say the son is much like
> both his father and mother.
> He will be listed prominently
> in the heroes of Óðin's family;
> the boy with the snake-eye
> will be the killer of many."

Ragnar took a golden ring from his hand and gave it to the boy as a naming-gift. And when Ragnar reached forward with the ring in his hand, the boy turned his back to him, and Ragnar took this as a sign that he would hate gold. And now he spoke this poem:

> "Brynhild's good grandson
> shows men that he has
> fierce shining eyes
> and the boldest of hearts.
> Buðli's great-grandson
> refuses a ring of pure gold;
> this early-blooming swordsman
> will be stronger than all men."

And then he spoke this:

> "I never saw
> brown serpents
> in the eyes of any boy,

except in Sigurð's alone.
He is easy to recognize,
this ungreedy boy,
he's sharp in the eye—
he's got a snake there."

Ragnar ordered his son to be taken back to Áslaug's room. This was the end of his plans to go to Sweden, and Áslaug's ancestry was revealed to everyone, so that they knew she was the daughter of Sigurð, the killer of Fáfnir, and of Brynhild, the daughter of Buðli.

Chapter 10. The Fall of Eirek and Agnar, and Áslaug's Demands

When the time came that Ragnar was supposed to come to the feast in Uppsala, and he did not come, King Eystein thought that this had been done to humiliate him and his daughter, and his friendship with King Ragnar ended. When Eirek and Agnar, Ragnar's sons, heard this, they discussed it and said that they ought to get together the biggest army they could and raid the Swedes. They assembled a great army and prepared their ships.

They thought it was important for their journey to have a good beginning. But it so happened that while Agnar's ship was launched from its rollers, a man was in its way, and he was killed. They called this "launch-blood," and it seemed to them that their journey was not beginning well, though they did not let it stand in their way.

When their troops were ready, they went to Sweden, and when they came into Eystein's kingdom they began to raid. When the Swedes saw this, they went to Uppsala and told King Eystein that an army had come into their land. The king had the war-arrow sent around his kingdom, and he assembled such a huge army that it was a wonder to look upon. He marched this army until he came into a certain forest, where he set up his tents. He had with him the cow Síbilja; many sacrifices had been made to the cow before it would come.

When they were in the forest, King Eystein said, "I have heard that Ragnar's sons are in the valleys beyond the forest, and it has been truthfully reported to me that they have less than a third of the troops that we have. Let's get all our troops ready for the fight, but send only a third out to meet them. Their troops are so tough that Ragnar's sons will think they are going to defeat us, and then suddenly we will come at them from all sides with the cow out in front of our army, and I don't think they'll be able to withstand the cow's moos."

This was done. And when the brothers saw this third part of Eystein's army, they didn't think they were going to be overpowered or outnumbered. And then suddenly the whole army came out of the forest, and the cow was let loose, and it ran in front of the troops and made terrible sounds. The noise was so bad that the soldiers who heard it fought among themselves, and only the two brothers were able to hold their ground.

The evil cow killed many men with its horns that day. And though Ragnar's sons were great men, they could not withstand both the superior numbers of their enemies and this sacrificial magic, but they put up a hard resistance and they defended themselves well and daringly, and with lasting fame. Eirek and Agnar were in the forefront of their army that day, and they often went through the ranks of King Eystein's soldiers.

Now Agnar was killed, and Eirek saw this and fought extremely boldly and did not care whether he escaped with his life or not. Then he was overcome and captured, and Eystein ordered the battle to be stopped, and he offered Eirek a truce. "And I will add this," said Eystein, "that I will marry my daughter to you."

Eirek spoke this poem:

> "I will accept no payment
> for my brother, nor a wife,
> nor hear Eystein named as
> the killer of Agnar.
> No mother mourns me,
> I am ready to die high above
> the other corpses here—
> let the spears pierce me."

Eirek said that he wanted his men to be spared and allowed to go wherever they wished. "But I want several spears to be taken and stood upright on the ground, and I want to be thrown on top of them and give up my life in that way."

Eystein said this would be done as he requested, though Eirek was choosing what was worse for them both. The spears were set up, and Eirek said:

> "No king's son
> I ever heard of
> died on a better bed
> for the raven's breakfast.
> The eager, thankless,
> shining-feathered bird
> will soon caw over
> both brothers' bodies."

Now Eirek went to where the spears were set, and he took a ring off his hand and threw it to his men who had been granted a truce, and he said it was for Áslaug. He added this poem:

> "Take these final words,
> my journey east is ended;
> tell the lovely lady Áslaug
> that she owns my rings now.
> She will be angry,
> my stepmother, when she hears
> I am dead; she will tell
> her gentle sons."

Then Eirek was heaved up onto the spears. He saw where a raven was flying, and he said:

> "The raven is hungry
> for my bloody head;
> that eager bird thirsts
> for my unseeing eyes.

You know, if the raven
pulls the eyes from my head,
that carrion-bird repays me badly
for the feasts I fed him."

Eirek then died with great courage. His messengers traveled home and did not let up until they came to where Ragnar had his throne. At the time, Ragnar was away at a meeting of kings, and his other sons had not yet come home from raiding.

The messengers stayed there three nights before they went to a meeting with Áslaug. When they went before Áslaug's throne, they greeted her nobly, and she accepted their greetings. She had her linen headdress resting on her knees, and she had loosened her hair and was about to comb it. She asked who these men were, because she had not seen them before. The foremost among them said that they had been in the army of Eirek and Agnar, the sons of Ragnar. Then she spoke this poem:

"What do you have to say?
Are the Swedes here,
or still in their land?
What's the news, king's man?
I have heard it told
that the Danes sailed north
after the 'launch-blood' omen,
but I heard nothing further."

The messenger said this in reply:

"I must tell you, woman,
Thóra's sons are dead—
fate has done evil
to your husband.
I know no bad news
newer than this.
Now the news is told,
an eagle flies over the fallen."

Áslaug asked how this had happened. The messenger told Áslaug the poem that Eirek had spoken when he sent the ring for her. The messengers saw that Áslaug shed a tear, and it was the color of blood and hard as a hailstone. No man before or since ever saw her weep.

Áslaug said that they could not undertake their revenge before Ragnar or his sons came home. "But you will stay here until then, and I will not hesitate to encourage vengeance for them as if they were my own sons."

The messengers remained there, and it happened that Ívar and his brothers came home before Ragnar, and they were not there long before Áslaug went to meet with her sons. Sigurd Snake-Eye was three years old at the time, and went with his mother. When the two of them came into the hall where the Ragnarssons held court, they greeted Áslaug well and they exchanged news. The brothers told of the death of Rognvald, her son, and about the other events that had happened. But she gave little attention to all this and she said:

> "My sons, you left me
> staring out to sea a long time.
> Now you've come home again;
> you come and go as you please.
> Battle-bold Rognvald,
> youngest of my sons,
> has gone to Ódin,
> reddened his shield with blood."

"I cannot see," she continued, "how he could have died better if he had lived longer."

The Ragnarssons asked Áslaug what news she had. She answered, "The deaths of your brothers Eirek and Agnar, my stepsons, two men I believe were the best kind of champions. It is not unusual that you find this intolerable and will avenge it terribly. And I want to help you in every way in getting revenge, so that we make it likely that they will be avenged too much rather than too little."

Ívar said, "I will certainly never go to Sweden and fight with King Eystein and the dark sacrifices there."

Áslaug adamantly opposed him, but Ívar was the leader of his brothers and he continued to refuse to go on this journey. Áslaug spoke this poem:

> "Your brothers
> would not have left you
> unavenged, not for
> even half a year,
> if you had died
> and Eirek and Agnar lived.
> They were not my sons—
> but I won't lie about this."

"I'm not sure," said Ívar, "that it helps at all, even if you say one poem after another. How do you know what kind of fortifications they have there?"

"I don't know," said Áslaug, "but what can you tell me about what kind of obstacles await us there?"

Ívar said that there were terrible sacrifices there, and that he had never heard of similar sacrifices anywhere. "And their king is both powerful and cruel."

"What is it that he makes most of his sacrifices to?"

Ívar said, "There is a huge cow they call Síbilja. This cow has the power to cause King Eystein's enemies to become powerless if they hear it mooing. Therefore we have not only men to fight against, but we must also anticipate that we will have to fight some dark magic before we can fight the king, and I wish to risk neither myself nor my troops there."

Áslaug said, "You must understand that you cannot both be called a great man, and also not take this risk." And when she decided that there was no point speaking to them any longer, she started to leave, thinking that they did not value her words at all.

Then Sigurd Snake-Eye said, "I will tell you, mother, something that occurs to me, but I cannot speak for my brothers."

"I want to hear what you have to say," she said. And then Sigurd Snake-Eye said this:

"If you are worried, mother,
it will take three nights
to make the navy ready;
we have a long voyage ahead.
If our swords are good,
Eystein will no longer be king
in Uppsala, no matter
how much he has sacrificed."

After he said this, his brothers began to change their minds some-what. And then Áslaug said, "Now, my son, you show that you want to do as I wish. But I do not think it is likely that just you and I can accomplish this ourselves if we don't have the assistance of your broth-ers. But it may be that we can get vengeance, and that would seem best to me. You please me, my son."

Bjorn now spoke this poem:

"There may be a brave heart
in a hawk-bold man's chest,
though the man stays silent
and keeps his own counsel.
I don't have any serpents
or glistening snakes in my eyes,
but my half-brothers cheered me,
and I remember them, your stepsons."

Then Hvítserk spoke this poem:

"Let's think, before we promise,
and let us rejoice
that Agnar's death
will be avenged.
Let us set sail,
break through the sea-ice,
see how fast our boats
can be made ready."

Hvítserk mentioned breaking through the sea-ice because there was a great deal of ice on the ocean, and their ships were pinned in by sheets of ice. And now Ívar said that he had been convinced to take some part in this, and he spoke this poem:

> "You all have great courage,
> you're not lacking in boldness—
> and together with that, we'll need
> plenty of toughness, too.
> Carry me at the head of the troops,
> brothers, boneless as I am,
> so that I can use both my hands
> in our battle for vengeance."

And Ívar added, "And now it has come to this, that we will apply as much courage as we are able in preparing the ships and gathering enough troops, because we will need everything we can get if we will be victorious."

And now Áslaug went away.

Chapter 11. The Attack by Áslaug and the Ragnarssons

Sigurd Snake-Eye had a foster-father, and this man had the ships prepared and the troops assembled in good order as a favor to Sigurd. And now the work went so swiftly that the troops Sigurd Snake-Eye wanted were made ready after only three nights had passed, and he had five ships, all of them well outfitted.

And after five nights had passed, Hvítserk and Bjorn had fourteen well-prepared ships. Ívar had ten ships prepared and Áslaug had another ten. Seven nights after they had discussed it and promised to make the journey, they all met together and reported to each other how many troops they had collected. Ívar reported that he had also sent a mounted regiment overland.

Áslaug said, "If I had thought that troops sent overland might make a difference, I would have sent a large number of them."

"Let's not dwell on it," said Ívar. "Let's depart with the troops we've gotten together."

Áslaug said that she wished to come with her sons, "And then I will see for myself how hard you try to avenge your brothers."

Ívar said, "You will certainly not come on our ships. But if you wish, you can lead the troops going overland."

Áslaug said that she would do so, and now her name was changed and she was called Randalín ever after.

Each of the divisions now departed, and Ívar told them where to meet. The journey went well for both groups, and they met at the appointed place. And wherever they went in Sweden in the kingdom of King Eystein, they raided and burned everything in their path. And they killed every human being and every other thing that breathed.

Chapter 12. The Fall of King Eystein

Now it happened that some men escaped and came to King Eystein, and told him that a great army had come into his kingdom, cruel men who were difficult to deal with and left nothing undone when it came to destroying everything in every place they went, and who left not one house standing.

When King Eystein heard this news, he thought he knew who these Vikings must be. He ordered the war-arrow sent all through his kingdom, calling to him all the men who owed him allegiance and wished to give him aid and who could hold a shield.

Eystein said, "We will take our goddess the cow Síbilja with us, and let her run at the front of the troops, and I suspect that it will go as before and they will be unable to stand her mooing. I will urge my troops to fight as best they can, and then we will rid ourselves of this large and menacing enemy army."

And now his orders were carried out, and Síbilja was let loose. Ívar saw the cow and heard its terrible mooing. He instructed all his troops to make a huge racket with their weapons and shouting, to drown out the noise made by the evil creature coming against them. Ívar told the men carrying him to take him as close to the cow as they could. "And when the cow comes at us, throw me onto it, and then either I will lose my life or I will kill the cow. And now take a large tree, and make a bow out of it and some arrows."

A large bow was made and brought to him together with some big arrows, and his men thought no one else would have been able to use such large weapons. Ívar encouraged each of his men to fight his hardest. The troops went forward with great ferocity and noise, and Ívar was carried forth ahead of all of them. There was such a loud noise made when Síbilja mooed that they heard it just as clearly as if they had been silent and stood at attention. The mooing drove all of the men insane, except the Ragnarssons, so much so that they wanted to fight among themselves.

While these monstrous things were happening, the men who were carrying Ívar saw him pulling back on his great bow as if it were nothing more than a flimsy elm branch, and having done so, they saw him put two arrows on it. And then they heard him shoot the arrows, and the bowstring snapped louder than they had ever heard. They saw that his arrows were flying out one after the other as fast as if they had been shot from the strongest crossbow, and they flew so true that each arrow hit Síbilja in a different eye. And now the cow fell, tumbling over headfirst, and its mooing became much worse than before.

The cow now came charging at them again, and Ívar told his men to throw him at the cow, and he seemed as light when they threw him as if he were a little child. They did not stand very close to the cow when they threw Ívar at it.

When Ívar landed on the back of the cow, he fell as heavily as a boulder would. Every bone inside the cow broke, and the cow met its death in this way.

Ívar ordered his men to pick him up as fast as they could. When they had picked him up, he spoke, and his voice carried so loudly that every man in the army felt that he was speaking to him directly even if he was far away, and they listened carefully to his instructions. As he ended his speech, his men who had been fighting one another stopped, and not much damage had been done as they had not been fighting one another long. Ívar encouraged them to fight as hard as they could against their enemies, and he said, "I think the worst part is past, since their cow is dead."

Now each side had regrouped its warriors, and they fell together in battle. The battle was so hard that all the Swedes swore they had never been in a harder trial by combat. The brothers Hvítserk and Bjorn pushed forward so hard that no enemy could stand against them. Such a large part of King Eystein's army was killed that only a minority were left standing, and some were in retreat. The battle ended with the death of King Eystein and the victory of Ragnar's sons. They spared whatever enemies of theirs were left alive.

Ívar said that he did not wish to raid any longer in this land now that it no longer had a ruler. "I would prefer if we went where we'd find more opposition," he said. And Randalín went home with some of their troops, but her son Sigurd Snake-Eye went with his brothers in every one of their raids afterwards.

Chapter 13. The Ragnarssons Take Vífilsborg

The Ragnarssons agreed that they would go raiding in the Southern Empire. In this expedition, they assaulted every large city that they came to and fought so hard that not one of them could withstand them. They soon learned of a city that was not only large and populous but also well defended. Ívar said that he wished to sail there. The names of this city and its ruler are told as follows: the chieftain was named Vífil, and the city was named Vífilsborg after him. The brothers went about attacking and destroying every city that lay between them and their objective until they came to the gates of Vífilsborg itself. The ruler was away from home, and he had taken a large army with him.

The brothers set up camp in the valleys outside the city, and one day they came to the city and spoke with its inhabitants, and they kept the peace that day. The Ragnarssons offered them either to give up their city willingly, in which case peace would be given to every inhabitant, or else to be conquered by superior arms and force, in which case no one would receive mercy.

But the city's defenders shot arrows at the Ragnarssons in reply, and they said that the brothers would never defeat the city or force its inhabitants to give it up. "First you would have to prove yourselves, and show us your boldness and valor."

The next night passed, and the day after, the Ragnarssons tried to take the city but failed. They laid siege to the city for half a month, and every day they tried to take it with various strategies. But they failed worse the longer they kept trying, and they began to think of giving up. When the inhabitants of Vífilsborg realized the Ragnarssons were near to giving up, they went out on the walls of their city and spread golden tapestries over all the walls, together with all the most beautiful fabrics they had in their city. On top of these they placed all their gold and the biggest jewels that were in their city. Then one of the men of Vífilsborg said, "We thought that these men, the Ragnarssons and their troops, were tough fighters, but now we can say they have not come any closer than others have." And after this the men of Vífilsborg hollered at them and beat on their shields and tried to provoke the Ragnarssons as best they could.

When Ívar heard this, it affected him so badly that he became sick and could not move, and his troops waited to see whether he would recover or die from his illness. He lay like this the entire day until evening, saying nothing. But then he ordered the men near him to tell Bjorn, Hvítserk, and Sigurð Snake-Eye that he wanted to see them and all the wisest men they had with them. And when the best leaders in the army had all come together, Ívar asked them if any of them had ideas that were more likely to succeed than those they had tried already.

But all of them said they were not clever enough to come up with a plan that might succeed. "As always, we'll have to follow your advice."

Then Ívar said, "One idea has occurred to me that we haven't tried. There is a large forest not far from here, and when night falls, we will secretly leave our tents and go into the forest, but leave our tents still standing behind us. And once we are in the forest, each one of us will take a load of firewood in his arms, and when this is done, we'll surround the city from every side and set fire to the wood we've gathered, and this will make a huge bonfire. The lime in the city walls will melt from the heat, and then we will take our catapults to the walls and see just how strong they are."

They did this, and they all went to the forest and spent as much time there as Ívar thought they needed. Then they went to the city, following

Ívar's plan, and when they set fire to their piles of firewood, it made such a large fire that the walls could not stand, and the lime in them melted out. Then the attackers went at the walls with their catapults and broke numerous holes in the sides, and a battle began. Now that they were fighting on more even terms, most of the city's defenders were killed, and some fled. The battle ended with the Ragnarssons and their army killing every human being who was in the city. Then they took all the valuables there, and they burned the city before they left.

Chapter 14. The Ragnarssons Raid in the Southern Empire

Now they traveled further on, until they came to a city called Luna. By this time they had destroyed nearly every city and fortress in the whole Southern Empire, and they had become so famous all across the world that there was no small child anywhere who did not know their name. They planned not to let up until they came to Rome itself, because they had heard that this city was great and populous and wonderful and rich. Yet they did not have a clear idea of how far it was, and they had such a large army that they could not feed their men.

They stopped at the city of Luna, and spoke among themselves about their expedition. A wise old man approached them then, and they asked him who he was. He said that he was a vagabond who had traveled widely his whole life.

"Then you will know a great deal of news to tell us about the things we want to know about."

The old man answered, "I doubt there are any lands you might want to ask about that I couldn't tell you about."

"We want you to tell us how far it is from here to Rome."

He said, "I can tell you something that will speak to this. Here you can see this pair of iron-soled shoes I have on my feet, and they are old, and this other worn-out pair I'm wearing across my back. When I left Rome, I had the shoes that are now on my back on my feet, and both pairs were new, and I have been on the road from there the whole time since."

When the old man had told them this, they thought they probably could not complete the journey they had intended to Rome. And so they turned away with their troops, and conquered many cities that had never been taken before, and the signs of their work remain to this day.

Chapter 15. The Death of King Ragnar in England

It is told that Ragnar sat at home in his kingdom and knew neither where his sons were nor where Randalín his wife was. But he heard all of his men saying that no one could be compared with his sons, and it seemed to him that no one was more famous than his sons had become. He began to think about what kind of great deed he might try to accomplish that might not achieve less fame.

He made up his mind at last, and hired shipmakers and ordered a forest of trees cut down to make two huge ships, and the people thereabouts saw that these would be two ocean-going warships so big that none of such size had ever been made before in Scandinavia. Ragnar also ordered every man in his entire kingdom to arm himself for war. And with that, people understood that Ragnar meant to leave the land on some raiding expedition. The news traveled widely across neighboring lands, and the people there and their rulers feared that they would be driven out of their lands and kingdoms. And every lord and chieftain ordered men to keep watch over his lands, in case anyone should attack.

And one time Randalín asked Ragnar what destination he intended to sail for. He told her that he intended to go to England, and to take with him no more ships than these two new large ships, and only as many troops as these could carry.

Randalín said, "This journey you're considering seems unwise to me. I think it would be wiser to bring smaller ships, but more of them."

"It's nothing special," said Ragnar, "if men conquer lands with many ships. But it's never been heard of before that such a land as England was conquered with just two ships. But if I am defeated, it will be all the better that I didn't take too many ships away from our land."

Randalín answered, "I don't think it would cost you more if you prepared many more longships for this journey before those two large ships are finished. And you know that it is difficult to sail near England. If it happens that your ships are lost, then your men are lost to you even if they do get to land, if an army shows up from the countryside. And it's easier to sail a longship than a large ocean-going ship into a harbor."

Then Ragnar spoke this poem:

> "A man shouldn't spare his gold
> if he wants his fighters' loyalty;
> an abundance of followers
> is better than an abundance of cash.
> It does no good to stand
> in the middle of a battle with golden rings.
> I've known many a rich man to die
> while his treasure survived him."

Now Ragnar ordered his ships made ready, and he assembled an army to fill his two ships. There was much talk about his plans. And now he spoke this poem:

> "What is this I hear
> echoing off the mountain walls,
> that the wise, generous warlord
> will sail his ships away?
> If the gods are willing, lady,
> the sea will rule the fate
> of the unfearing man,
> and receive his gold."

Once his ships were ready, together with his troops, and once the weather had turned favorable, Ragnar said that he would board his ships. When he was ready, Randalín went with him to his ships. Before they parted, she said that she would loan him the shirt he had given her. He asked what kind of shirt this was. She replied with this poem:

"With my whole heart,
I give you this long shirt:
it is of one piece, woven
from a single long, gray hair.
No wound will bleed you,
no blade will bite you
in this holy armor—
it was blessed by the gods."

Ragnar said that he would accept it. And as they parted, it was clear to see that saying farewell weighed heavily on Randalín.

Ragnar then sailed his ships to England, as he had intended. The winds were fierce, and as he drew near to England both of his ships wrecked, and all his troops were driven to shore in their armor and weapons. And in England, wherever he came to a farm or town or castle, Ragnar had the victory.

There was a king named Ella who ruled England at this time. He had heard about Ragnar when he left on his expedition. He had set men to watch so that he would know if the army came to land in England. These men came to Ella now and told him about the army. Ella had his orders sent all throughout his kingdom, commanding every man to come to him who could hold a shield and ride a horse and who dared to fight. He assembled such a large army that it was an amazing sight. Ella and his men now prepared for battle, and King Ella said to his men: "If we win this battle, and you notice that Ragnar is within sight, do not attack him with weapons, because he has sons who will never let us forget him if he is killed."

Ragnar prepared for battle, and instead of his armor he was wearing the shirt that Randalín had given him when they parted, and in his hand he had the spear that he had used to kill the dragon—the one that once had lived encircling Thóra's hall, and that no one but Ragnar had dared to fight, when he had nothing to protect himself except a helmet.

The battle began when the two armies met, and Ragnar had a much smaller force. The battle had not gone on long before a large number of Ragnar's troops had fallen. But wherever Ragnar himself went, he cleared his path of all the enemies who stood before him, and he went straight through the enemy ranks that day, and wherever he cut or stabbed at someone's shield, armor, or helmet, his blows were so strong that no living thing could withstand him. But he himself was never shot or cut, and no weapon injured him and he was not harmed in any way, even while he killed a great number of the troops of King Ella. But the battle ended with the death of all of Ragnar's men, and Ragnar himself was hemmed in with shields and captured.

Now they asked Ragnar who he was, but he was silent and answered nothing.

Then King Ella said, "This man must have been through some tougher tests than this, if he won't tell us his name. Throw him into a pit full of snakes and let him sit there a while, and if he says anything that indicates he may be Ragnar, we will take him out immediately."

So Ragnar was let down into a serpent-pit, and he sat there a long time while none of the snakes would bite him. And some people said, "This is a great man; no weapons would bite him today, and now the serpents will not bite him."

Then King Ella ordered them to remove the outermost layer of clothes he was wearing, and this was done. And now the snakes stuck their fangs into every part of him.

Ragnar said, "How the piglets would squeal, if they knew what the old boar was going through." And even though he said this, they did not understand for certain yet that this was Ragnar and not some other king. But then Ragnar spoke this poem:

> "I have fought battles
> that men called glorious—
> I count fifty-one—
> and I've killed many men.
> I never expected
> that worms would kill me,
> but often what happens
> is what we're least prepared for."

And he continued with this poem:

> "How the piglets would squeal
> if they saw the old boar now!

The serpents bite deep,
and my injuries are grim.
The vipers have struck hard
and sucked my blood.
It's not long till I'm a corpse,
lying dead among these beasts."

Then Ragnar died, and he was carried away from that place. King Ella now considered it likely that it was Ragnar who had died here, and he contemplated how he could find out for certain, and how he could hold on to his kingdom, and how Ragnar's sons would react when they learned of this.

Ella accepted a suggestion to prepare a ship, and to assign to it a captain who was known to be both wise and tough, and to assign further men to the ship so that it would have a solid crew. He said he would send this crew to meet with Ívar and his brothers and to tell them of the death of Ragnar, their father. But this journey sounded unpleasant to most men, and there were few who wished to undertake it.

The king told the men who were to go on this journey: "Pay attention to how each of the Ragnarssons reacts when the news is told. Then come back, when the weather is with you." Then he ordered them to prepare for their journey, so that nothing would be lacking. Then they left, and their voyage went well.

At this time the sons of Ragnar had been raiding in the Southern Empire. They returned to Scandinavia and intended to visit the kingdom where Ragnar ruled. But they knew nothing of his latest expedition, or what had happened on it, and they were very curious to know how it had gone.

The Ragnarssons sailed north, and wherever people heard that they were coming, they destroyed their own cities and took their movable property and fled away, so that the Ragnarssons could hardly feed their own army.

One morning, Bjorn Ironside woke up and spoke this poem:

"Every morning a raven
flies over these cities,
loudly calling, acting

like he'll die of hunger;
but let him fly south,
over the sands where we left
wounded men, there he'll drink
the blood of blade-killed men."

And then he spoke this:

"When we first left home,
when we began making battles,
and fought hard with our enemies,
we went into Roman lands.
I drew my sword, let the eagle
scream over the corpses
of the murdered, while
my mustache turned gray."

Chapter 16. Concerning the Ragnarssons and King Ella

Now it is told that the Ragnarssons returned to Denmark before King Ella's messengers came, and they rested there with their troops. But the messengers soon arrived with their own followers, at a time when the Ragnarssons were holding a feast. The messengers went into the hall where they were drinking, and stood before the throne where Ívar was sitting. Sigurd Snake-Eye and Hvítserk the Bold were sitting and playing *hnefatafl* [a board game], while Bjorn Ironside sat on the floor, where he was shaving a spearshaft smooth.

When Ella's messengers came before Ívar, they greeted him formally. He received their greeting and asked them where they had come from and what sort of news they might have to tell. The foremost among the messengers said that they were Englishmen and that King Ella had sent them to tell the news of the death of Ragnar, their father.

Hvítserk and Sigurd stopped in the middle of their game and listened carefully to hear the news. Bjorn stood up from the floor and leaned on his spear.

Ívar asked the messengers carefully about every detail of how Ragnar had lost his life. They told him everything that had happened from the time when Ragnar came to England to the moment when he died. And when they were finished telling the story, with the last words Ragnar had spoken—"How the piglets would squeal"—Bjorn slid his hand down the spearshaft, and he had been gripping it so hard that the marks from his finger-grips remained. And at the moment the messengers finished their story, Bjorn shook his spear so hard that it broke in two. Meanwhile Hvítserk was holding a game piece he had captured, and he squeezed it so hard that blood gushed out from under every fingernail. Sigurd Snake-Eye had been using a knife to trim his fingernails while the story was told. He listened so intently that he did not notice he was cutting himself with it until it sliced all the way to the bone, but he did not show any sign that he felt it.

And Ívar asked for every detail, and his face turned sometimes red, sometimes blue, sometimes pale, and he was so swollen that all his flesh seemed inflated from the grimness in his heart.

Hvítserk spoke up now, and said their vengeance should begin immediately with the killing of King Ella's messengers.

Ívar said, "That won't happen. They will leave here in peace, and go wherever they please, and if they lack anything they need, they can tell me and I will get it for them."

When the messengers had completed their errand, they left the hall and returned to their ship. And when the wind was in their favor, they sailed away and had a good voyage until they came back to King Ella and told him how each of Ragnar's sons had reacted to hearing this news told.

When King Ella heard this, he said: "I expect we need to fear either Ívar or none of them, based on what you have told me about him. The others have brave hearts, but we could hold our kingdom against them." He ordered watchmen to be posted all over his kingdom, so that no invading army could surprise him.

Meanwhile, when King Ella's messengers were gone, the Ragnarssons met for a conference to discuss how they might avenge their father Ragnar.

Ívar said, "I will have no part in this, and I will contribute no soldiers, because what happened to Ragnar was what I expected. From the beginning, he was badly unprepared for what he undertook to do. He had no quarrel with King Ella, and it has often happened that a man who is too proud and deals unrighteously with others is brought down shamefully. I will accept money in compensation for our father from King Ella, if he will offer it to me."

His brothers were furious when they heard this, and said they would never let themselves be disgraced in this way, even if Ívar did. "And many men would say that we didn't know how to act rightly, if we left our father's death unavenged, considering that we have gone raiding all around the world and killed many a man without cause. No, that shall not be. We will prepare every seaworthy ship in Denmark, and gather such a great army that every man who can take up a shield against King Ella will go with us."

But Ívar said that he would stay out of it together with all the ships that he had command over, "except for the one I call my own."

When it became known that Ívar would give no aid to this expedition, they were able to gather a much smaller army than otherwise, but in spite of this they did not hesitate to set out. And when they reached England, King Ella heard of their arrival and ordered the trumpet blown to summon everyone who would follow him. He gathered such a large army that no one could count their number, and he marched against the Ragnarssons. The two armies met, and Ívar was not present for that battle. The confrontation ended with the Ragnarssons driven away, and King Ella took the victory.

And while the king was driving their army away, Ívar said that he had no intent of going back to his own land, "And I will see whether King Ella will do me some honor, or not, and I think it will be better to accept payment from him than continue with such failed expeditions like the one we've just been on."

Hvítserk said that he would have nothing to do with him, and that Ívar could do whatever he wanted for his part, "But we will never accept payment from him for our father."

Ívar told him they would say farewell with that said, and he asked the others to rule their shared kingdom, "And you must send me the amount of money that I determine." And when he had told them this, he said farewell, and he turned back to meet King Ella.

When Ívar came before King Ella, he greeted the king respectfully and began his speech in this way: "I have come to meet with you, and

I want to make a settlement with you and accept whatever honors you will give me. I see now that I have no reason to fight against you, and I think it's better to accept whatever honors you want to give me than risk the death of more of my men, or of my own self."

King Ella answered, "Some people say that it's impossible to trust you, and that you often speak well when you intend to break your word. It is difficult for me to believe you, or your brothers."

"I will ask you for only very little, if you will grant my request. And I will swear to you in turn that I will never stand against you."

King Ella asked him what he wanted in payment.

"I want," said Ívar, "for you to give me only as much of your own land as a steer-hide will cover, though outside of that I will be permitted to lay a building's foundation as well. I will not ask for more from you, and if you will not grant this request, I will think you want to give me no honor whatsoever."

The king said, "I don't know whether this will harm me in some way, if you take this piece from my land, but I will certainly give it to you if you will swear not to fight against me. I do not fear your brothers, as long as *you* are true to me."

Chapter 17. King Ella Is Killed

Now King Ella and Ívar agreed to this, and Ívar swore oaths to Ella to the effect that he would never fire an arrow against Ella and never give counsel that would lead to harm for him, and that in return he would receive land in England that was as large as the biggest steer-hide Ívar could find might cover.

Ívar went and got a hide from an old bull, and he gave orders for the hide to be softened and stretched three times. Then he had it cut into the thinnest possible strips, and he had the hair-side split from the flesh-side. When this was done, it formed a string so long that it was amazing to look at; no one had imagined that it would come out so long. Then he gave orders for it to be spread across a certain plain, and there were such vast lands there that it could have held a large city, and outside of this territory he had marked out, he also laid out a foundation that would suit a large fortress with walls. Then he gathered together several skilled builders and ordered many houses to be built on this plain, as well as a large city that is called London. That is the largest and most excellent of all cities in Scandinavia.

When Ívar had finished building this city, he had spent all his money. He was so generous that he gave money away with both hands, and his wisdom was considered so great that everyone went to him with problems to seek his advice. And he settled every dispute that was brought to him in a way that seemed to be to everyone's advantage, and he became so popular that he was regarded as a friend by all. Ívar was a great help to King Ella in every issue that concerned the ruling of his kingdom, and Ella let him decide about many matters and disputes as his representative when the king himself could not be present.

And when Ívar had established himself with his famed wisdom, he sent messengers to his brothers, asking them to send him as much gold and silver as he demanded. When the messengers came to his brothers, they explained their mission and everything Ívar had accomplished, because they did not know what Ívar's plan was. His brothers understood that Ívar's mood had not changed too much from normal, and they sent him all the money that he demanded.

When the messengers came back to Ívar, he gave all the money to the greatest men in the land, and in this way he siphoned support away from King Ella. All of them swore that they would keep the peace even if Ívar marched an army in their direction.

When Ívar had gathered this much support, he sent messengers to his brothers to tell them that he wanted them to conscript an army from all the lands where they had power, and to call up every soldier they could. When this message came to his brothers, they understood right away that Ívar thought it was likely that they would be victorious. They gathered an army from every part of Denmark and Götaland and all the realms where they held power, and they assembled an invincible army and then led their conscripts out of the country. They sailed their ships toward England night and day, wishing to make it difficult for their enemies to see them coming.

This was told to King Ella. He assembled an army, but he was able to find few fighters, because Ívar had siphoned away so much of his support.

Now Ívar went to the king and said that he would keep the promise that he had sworn, "But I have no control over what my brothers do. Still, I will go to them and find out whether they will halt their army and agree to do no more harm than they have already done."

Ívar went to his brothers and gave them a great deal of provocation, telling them to get started as best they could and let the battle come as soon as possible, because King Ella had a much smaller army. His brothers answered that Ívar had no need to egg them on like this, because they had the same intentions as before.

Ívar went back to King Ella and told him that his brothers were too wild and crazed to want to listen to him, "And when I tried to propose a peace between them and you, they yelled at me and rejected it. Still, *I* will keep my promise not to fight against you, and I will stay peaceably out of the battle with my own men. But the battle between them and you will go as it will."

Now King Ella saw the army of the Ragnarssons, and the troops came forward so ferociously that they were a marvel to look upon. Ívar said, "King Ella, it is time to call up your army, but I think that my brothers will give you a hard battle for a little while."

As soon as the two armies met, there was a great battle. The Ragnarssons attacked hard, and pushed through the ranks of King Ella's troops; they were so furious that they thought only about dealing out as much injury as they could, and the fight was long and hard. And it ended with King Ella and his army driven into retreat, and King Ella was captured.

Then Ívar came, and he said they needed to find an appropriate death for King Ella. "It would be wise," he said, "to remember the kind of death he gave our father. Let's have a man who's good with a knife cut an eagle deep in his back, and color the eagle red with his blood."

The man who was chosen for this work did as Ívar commanded, and King Ella was horrifically wounded before this task was done. Then Ella died, and the Ragnarssons felt that they had avenged their father Ragnar.

Ívar said that he would give his brothers the whole kingdom they had owned together, but that he would keep England for himself.

Chapter 18. The End of the Ragnarssons

After this, Hvítserk, Bjorn, and Sigurd Snake-Eye went home to their own kingdom, but Ívar stayed behind and ruled over England. From that point on, they kept a smaller army, but they continued to raid in various lands. Their mother Randalín became an old woman.

Hvítserk raided one time in the east, and there he was faced with such a larger force that he could barely raise a shield against his enemies, and he was captured. He chose to die by being burned on a pile of men's severed heads, and he was killed in this way. When Randalín heard about this, she spoke this poem:

> "One of the sons I had,
> the one named Hvítserk,
> has endured death in the east;
> he was never inclined to flee.
> He was burned on a pile of heads
> cut from men killed in battle;
> that bold lord of men chose
> that death, before he fell dead."

And then she said:

> "They piled up a heap
> of hundreds of men's heads
> under a great man, my doomed son,
> and let the flames roar up;
> what better bed could a warrior
> have chosen to sleep on?
> That powerful man dies
> with honor; it's a lord who falls."

A great family is descended from Sigurd Snake-Eye. His daughter was Ragnhild, the mother of Harald Fair-Hair, who was the first king to rule all of Norway.

As for Ívar, he ruled England until his death-day, and he died of sickness. And while he lay in his final sickness, he ordered his body to be taken to the place where a raiding army would land, and he said he expected that they would not win the victory when they came ashore. When he died, it was done as he commanded, and he was buried in a mound there. Many people say that when King Harald Hard-Ruler came to England, he landed where Ívar was buried, and he was killed in that expedition. And when William the Conqueror came to England, he went to Ívar's mound and broke it open, and there he saw Ívar's body undecomposed. William had a bonfire built and then burned Ívar's body on that pyre, and after that he fought for the rule of the kingdom and he won it.

Bjorn Ironside also has many descendants. A great family is descended from him, such as Thórd, a great chieftain who lived at the farm named Höfði á Höfðaströnd.

When all the Ragnarssons were dead, their former followers drifted away in various directions. For a man who had served under the Ragnarssons, no other leader seemed to be worth anything. There were two men in particular who traveled widely around many lands searching, each one of them on his own, for any man they would not be ashamed to be led by.

Chapter 19. Concerning King Ragnar's Men

The news traveled through many lands that a king had two sons. This king became ill and he died, and his sons wanted to drink to their inheritance from him. They planned a feast in three years' time, and invited everyone to come who heard about it in the next three years. Over these three years, they prepared the feast. And when the summer came when the feast was to be held, and the appointed time arrived, there was such a huge crowd that no one could guess how many guests there were, and many large halls were prepared and many tents besides.

When most of the first evening had passed, a man came to one of these halls. He was so big that no one else there was as large, and from the clothing he wore, anyone could tell that he had been in the company of noble men. When he came into the hall, he went before the brothers and greeted them and asked them where they would let him sit. They liked the look of him, and asked him to sit at the high-est bench. He took up as much space as two men. When he had sat down, drinks were brought to him as they were to the other men, but there was no drinking horn so large that he could not drink it dry in one gulp. Everyone thought this man seemed unimpressed by all the other men there.

But then it happened that a second man came to this feast. He was even larger than the first. Both these men wore long-brimmed hats. And when the second man came before the throne of the young kings, he greeted them elegantly and asked them where they would let him sit. They said that this man ought to sit closer to them, on the highest bench. He went to his seat, and together with the other stranger who had come in, he displaced five men. And this second stranger was even more of a drinking man than the first. He drank so fast that he simply seemed to pour each horn's contents down his throat, though no one thought he seemed drunk. He was not friendly to the men sitting near him, and he showed his back to them.

The first man who had come in said that they should have some fun together, and he said, "I'll go first." He gestured at the other man with his hand, and spoke this poem:

> "Tell us about your heroism,
> I ask you: where did you see
> the blood-drunk raven
> calling from a branch?
> I think you've more often
> accepted drinks at other feasts
> than laid out bodies on the plain
> and set a table for the ravens."

The other man felt offended by such slander and he composed this poem in reply:

> "Shut up, you dumb stay-at-home,
> they call you a lazy little man—
> you've never done anything
> that I couldn't do better.

I never saw you in battle,
—not even in sunshine!—
you've never killed for the wolves;
your only business is drinking."

The first man answered in this way:

"We let our ships sail
the waves of the great sea,
and we made bloody wounds
in men with shining armor.
The she-wolf howled,
and the eagle felt his hunger
satisfied on a man's neck.
We took gold, and drew blood."

And now the second man spoke:

"I never saw any of you
when we sailed the open sea
for miles on a white-sailed
ocean-going ship, and when,
at the sound of the trumpets,
we launched, setting sail,
and before our blood-red prow
we gave rich gifts to the raven."

Then the first man said this:

"It's not fitting for us two
to argue at this feast
about what each of us did
better than the other;
you stood where waves crashed
against the ship at sea,
and I sat where the sailyard
turned the red ship to harbor."

Then the second man said:

> "We both followed Bjorn—
> and sometimes Ragnar—
> into every battle;
> men were tested hard.
> I was there for the battle
> that broke out in Bulgaria;
> I was injured there, in my side.
> Sit closer in, comrade."

Now the two men recognized each other again, and they remained at the feast.

Chapter 20. Concerning Ogmund the Dane

A man was named Ogmund, who was called Ogmund the Dane. He sailed once with five ships, and he anchored off the island Samsø in the harbor at Munarvág. It is told that his servants went ashore to prepare food, while some of his other men went to the woods to enjoy themselves. There they found an old wooden idol shaped like a man, forty feet high and grown over with moss, though they could see every side of it clearly. They talked about who could have sacrificed to this great god. Then the wooden man said:

> "It was long ago,
> Høkling's sons
> sailed their ships
> far away from here.
> They drove ships
> over the ocean,
> and I was the lord
> of this village.

> "The warriors,
> sons of Lodbrók,

set me up
south of the sea.
On the south end
of Samsø,
they sacrificed to me
for victory in war.

"They told me to stand
while the island lasts,
a man covered
in thorns and moss.
The rain wets me,
and I am covered
by neither flesh
nor clothing."

The men were amazed at this, and they told others about it later.

Glossary of Names and Terms

A **[V]** in brackets is printed after names that appear in the Saga of the Volsungs, and an **[R]** after names that appear in the Saga of Ragnar Loðbrók. Names that appear in both are marked **[V, R]**.

Note that the alphabetization of this glossary is based on American rather than Scandinavian conventions. Æ is treated as A+E, Ð is treated as D, Ø and (in Swedish and Modern Icelandic placenames) Ö are treated as O, Ǫ is printed as and treated as O, and Þ is printed as and alphabetized as TH. The length of vowels is printed but ignored in alphabetization. More details on the anglicization of Old Norse used in this volume can be found in the Introduction.

Where poems of the Poetic Edda are referenced, their titles are printed in Old Norse following this volume's conventions, and then in parentheses in the more anglicized form in which they appear in *The Poetic Edda: Stories of the Norse Gods and Heroes* (Hackett, 2015).

Æsir [V], the principal family of the Norse gods, including Óðin, Thór, Frigg, and Týr.

Agnar (1) [V], a king who fought Hjálm-Gunnar with Brynhild's support.

Agnar (2) [R], a son of Ragnar Loðbrók and Thóra (2).

Aki [R], a peasant farmer, husband of Gríma, and foster-father of Áslaug/Kráka.

Álf (1) [V], a son of Hunding, killed by Helgi.

Álf (2) [V], a Danish king and the second husband of Hjordís, after the death of Sigmund (1). He rules alongside his father Hjálprek.

Alsvid [V], son of Heimir and Bekkhild, who acts as a friend and host to Sigurd when he visits Heimir.

Andvaranaut [V], a ring formerly belonging to the dwarf known as Andvari. It is cursed to become the death of anyone who possesses it.

Andvari [V], a dwarf who lives in the form of a fish. Loki takes his treasure and the ring Andvaranaut.

Andvari's Falls [V], the waterfall where Andvari dwells.

Ásgard [V], the realm where the Norse gods dwell.

Áslaug [V, R], daughter of Brynhild and Sigurd. She is mentioned only once in the Saga of the Volsungs (in chapter 27, when Brynhild puts her in the care of Heimir), but she becomes a major character in the Saga of Ragnar Lodbrók. After she is taken to Norway by Heimir, she is raised there by Aki and Gríma, who rename her Kráka ("Crow"), and she does not reveal her true name until she has been married to Ragnar for many years, when she is pregnant with Sigurd Snake-Eye. She later changes her name once again, to Randalín, when she goes with her sons to avenge Eirek and Agnar (2) on Eystein.

Atli [V], king of Hunland, the son of Budli and brother of Brynhild and Oddrún. He is the second husband of Gudrún, whose brothers Gunnar and Hogni he later kills. Although based distantly on the historical Attila the Hun, there is little connection between the saga character and the historical Hunnish leader.

Audi [V], mentioned by Brynhild as the brother of Agnar (1).

Barnstokk [V], a tree, called an oak tree in chapter 2 of the Saga of the Volsungs, and an apple tree in chapter 3. It grows in the middle of Volsung's hall, where Ódin places the sword Gram in it during the wedding of Siggeir and Signý. The name of the tree can be interpreted as "family tree."

Bekkhild [V], a sister of Brynhild and Atli, mentioned only in passing as the wife of Heimir.

Bikki [V], a counselor in the service of Jormunrekk.

Bjorn Ironside [R], a son of Ragnar Lodbrók and Áslaug.

Borghild [V], first wife of Sigmund (1). Sigmund banishes her for killing Sinfjotli.

Brávellir [V, R], site of a legendary battle between Sigurd Ring and Harald Wartooth, and also mentioned as the site of a horse race by Sinfjotli.

Bredi [V], a slave owned by Skadi.

Brynhild [V, R], a Valkyrie. She is the daughter of Budli, the sister of Atli, Oddrún, and Bekkhild, and the foster-daughter of her sister Bekkhild's husband Heimir. She becomes the mother of Áslaug (with Sigurd) and the wife of Gunnar.

Busiltjorn [V], a river or pond that Sigurð and an old man (Óðin in disguise) drive horses into, in order to determine which horse should be Sigurð's. The text states that it is a river, although *tjorn* means "pond."

Buðli [V, R], father of Atli, Oddrún, Bekkhild, and Brynhild (the latter is frequently called "the daughter of Buðli").

Denmark [V, R], roughly coterminous with the modern country, but in the medieval period it included much of what is now southern Sweden.

Dwarf [V], a mythical, humanlike creature (Old Norse *dvergr*). Dwarves are represented as master craftsmen, and many of them have shape-changing abilities (for instance, Andvari lives as a fish and Otter as an otter) and the power to enter solid stone in order to hide themselves. Hreiðmar and his children (including Fáfnir, Otter, and Regin) are not explicitly called dwarves in the Saga of the Volsungs, although the word is used for Regin in the Poetic Edda.

Eirek [R], a son of Ragnar Loðbrók and his first wife Thóra (2).

Eitil [V], son of Atli and Guðrún. Together with his brother Erp (1), he is killed by Guðrún.

Elf [V], a creature (Old Norse *álfr*) mentioned sometimes in Norse mythology in association with the gods, but never described. It is possible that elves were the same kind of creature as dwarves.

Ella [R], king of Northumbria in England (though represented as king of all England in the saga) and killer of Ragnar Loðbrók. The Ragnarssons avenge their father by having a man "cut an eagle deep in his back," a torture which, in elaborated form, has become somewhat famous under the name of the "blood eagle."

England [R], roughly coterminous with the modern country in Great Britain, though it was not one unified kingdom during the early Middle Ages.

Erp (1) [V], son of Atli and Guðrún. Together with his brother Eitil, he is killed by Guðrún.

Erp (2) [V], son of Jónakr and Guðrún, murdered by his brothers Hamðir and Sorli. According to the very old poem *Hamðismál* (*Hamthismal*) in the Poetic Edda, he is the son of Jónakr and a concubine, and in that earlier source his murder by his half-brothers seems to have something to do with his lower status and their distrust of him as an illegitimate son.

Eyjólf [V], a son of Hunding, killed by Helgi.

Eylimi [V], a king, father of Hjordís and Grípir and thus Sigurð's father-in-law.

Eymód [V], mentioned as a companion of Gunnar when he goes to Guðrún after the murder of Sigurð.

Eystein [R], a legendary king of Sweden, father of Ingibjorg who is briefly Ragnar Loðbrók's fiancée. He kills Agnar (2) and Eirek, and later does battle with the surviving sons of Ragnar.

Family spirits [V], used as a translation of Old Norse *(spá)dísir*, which refers to female spirits who may act as guardians of the living members of a family, or appear in dreams to warn them of coming troubles.

Fáfnir [V, R], the dragon slain by Sigurd. Fáfnir is the brother of Regin and Otter, and seems to become a dragon only after he kills their father Hreidmar.

Fjornir [V], a servant of Gunnar.

Franks [V], an early medieval Germanic tribe.

Frekastein [V], location of the battle between Helgi and Hoðbrodd.

Frigg [V], a goddess, wife of Óðin.

Fyn [V], a major island in Denmark.

Gaulnir [V], a giant alluded to by Sinfjotli when he insults Granmar (2).

German [V], the language of Germany, as distinct from the larger subfamily of Germanic languages (which includes Old and Modern English, Gothic, Old Norse, and the modern Scandinavian languages). German is referred to by name in chapter 32 of the Saga of the Volsungs, when it is said that Sigurd's name will be famous forever in the German language and in Scandinavia.

Giant [V], traditional English translation of Old Norse *jotunn*, a family of beings who are usually portrayed as enemies of the gods. In spite of the conventional translation as "giant," they are not necessarily huge, and the giants do not typically seem to look different from the gods and humans they interact with. Hrímnir, the father of Hljóð (and thus father-in-law of Volsung and grandfather of Sigmund), is said to be a giant in the Saga of the Volsungs.

Gjúki [V], father of Gunnar, Hogni (2), and Guttorm, and husband of Grímhild.

Gjúkung [V], a term for descendants of Gjúki, especially his sons.

Glaumvor [V], second wife of Gunnar. She has prophetic dreams.

Gnitaheid [V], the place where the dragon Fáfnir dwells with his treasure.

Gnípafjord [R], a fjord associated with the city Hvítabø.

Gnípalund [V], a harbor.

Götaland [V, R], a region of modern Sweden that was once politically distinct from Sweden proper; in Old English its people were called "Geats" (Beowulf, famously, was a Geat). In the Saga of the Volsungs, Siggeir is represented as its king. In the Saga of Ragnar Lodbrók, Herrud rules at least part of Götaland, and it is later claimed by Ragnar. *Götaland* is the Swedish spelling that can be found on modern maps; the Old Norse spelling is *Gautland*.

Goth [V], a Germanic people of late antiquity and the early Middle Ages.

Goti [V], Gunnar's stallion.

Gram [V], the name given to the broken sword of Sigmund (1) after Regin reforges it for Sigurd.

Grani [V], Sigurd's stallion. This is not an unusual name for a horse; it means "whiskery." The father of Grani is Sleipnir, the stallion of the god Ódin, who is associated with the color gray. Sinfjotli also mentions a stallion named Grani when he is insulting Granmar (2), but there is no reason to think that this is the same Grani as Sigurd's.

Granmar (1) [V], father of Hodbrodd and Granmar (2).

Granmar (2) [V], brother of Hodbrodd, who exchanges insults with Sinfjotli.

Gríma [R], a peasant farmer, and wife of Aki. After causing the death of Heimir, she becomes the foster-mother of Áslaug/Kráka.

Grímhild [V], a witch, and the wife of Gjúki and mother of Gunnar, Hogni (2), Gudrún, and Guttorm.

Grindr [V], a location mentioned in connection with Helgi's forces.

Grípir [V], brother of Hjordís who is capable of seeing the future.

Gunnar [V], son of Gjúki and Grímhild, oldest brother of Guttorm, Gudrún, and Hogni (2). He marries Brynhild after Sigurd courts her in the disguise of Gunnar.

Gudrún [V], sister of Guttorm, Gunnar, and Hogni (2). With her first husband Sigurd, she is the mother of Sigmund (2) and Svanhild.

With her second husband Atli, she is the mother of Erp (1) and Eitil (2). With her third husband Jónakr, she is mother of Hamdir, Sorli, and Erp (2).

Guttorm [V], youngest brother of Gudrún, Gunnar, and Hogni (2), and killer of Sigurd.

Hagbard (1) [V], a son of Hunding, killed by Helgi.

Hagbard (2) [V], a son of Hámund.

Haki [V], a son of Hámund.

Hákon [V], father of Thóra (1).

Hálf [V], the Danish king whose hall Gudrún lives at after the murder of Sigurd. He may originally have been meant to be the same person as Álf (2).

Hamdir [V], son of Gudrún and Jónakr, brother of Sorli and Erp (2), and half-brother of Svanhild.

Hámund [V], second son of Sigmund (1) and Borghild. It is unclear whether he might be the same Hámund mentioned by Brynhild in passing in chapter 25.

Harald Fairhair [R], historical first king of unified Norway; he died ca. AD 933. As the son of Ragnhild, he is represented in the Saga of Ragnar Lodbrók as the grandson of Sigurd Snake-Eye.

Harald Hard-Ruler [R], historical king of Norway; he died in AD 1066 in a failed attempt to conquer England.

Harald Wartooth [R], legendary early king of Denmark.

Hedinsey [V], an island.

Heimir [V, R], foster-father of Brynhild and husband of her sister Bekkhild. Brynhild lives with him before she marries Gunnar. The Saga of Ragnar Lodbrók tells that Heimir flees with Brynhild's daughter Áslaug to Norway after the death of Brynhild.

Hel [V], the underworld to which most people are committed for the afterlife. According to the classic understanding of Norse mythology, men who die in battle go to Valhalla instead, but the phrase "sending someone to Hel" may be used for killing someone in any context.

Helgi [V], a son of Sigmund (1) and Borghild. His story is passed over quickly in chapters 8 and 9 of the Saga of the Volsungs, but three poems are devoted to him in the Poetic Edda.

Herrud [R], a jarl in Götaland, father of Thóra (2).

Hervard [V], a son of Hunding, killed by Helgi.

Hild [V], a common element in women's names (e.g., Brynhild, Svanhild). It literally means "battle."

Hindarfjall [V], the mountain where Brynhild is imprisoned when Sigurd first meets her.

Hjalli [V], a slave in Atli's realm.

Hjálm-Gunnar [V], a king killed by Brynhild, in defiance of Ódin's orders.

Hjálprek [V], father of Álf (2). He shares the rule of the Danish kingdom with his son.

Hjordís [V], second wife of Sigmund (1) and mother of Sigurd. After the death of Sigmund, she is remarried to Álf (2).

Hjorvard [V], a son of Hunding.

Hljód [V], the Valkyrie sent by Ódin to Rerir to give him a magic apple allowing him to conceive a child. She later marries Rerir's son Volsung.

Hlymdalir [V, R], the domain of Heimir.

Hodbrodd [V], Helgi's rival for the hand of Sigrún.

Höfdi á Höfdaströnd [R], a real farm in north-central Iceland on the east shore of the large fjord Skagafjördur. It is said the farm was settled by Thórd, a descendant of Ragnar Lodbrók.

Hogni (1) [V], father of Sigrún.

Hogni (2) [V], brother of Guttorm, Gunnar, and Gudrún. He is represented as a supremely capable warrior, and as the most honorable and reasonable of his brothers.

Holkvir [V], the stallion of Hogni (2).

Hönir [V], a poorly known god, mentioned as a companion of Ódin and Loki in Regin's story about the origin of Fáfnir's treasure. Aside from occurring in the story of Fáfnir's treasure, he is mentioned only incidentally in the Poetic Edda in the story of the creation of humans and then as one of the few survivors of Ragnarok (the end of the world when most of the gods will be killed).

Hreidmar [V], the father of Fáfnir, Otter, and Regin. He is killed by Fáfnir.

Hrímnir [V], a giant, and the father of the Valkyrie named Hljód.

Hring [V], an ally of Hodbrodd.

Hringstadir [V], a location associated with the Volsungs.

Hrotti [V], a sword.

Hun [V], an Asian people of late antiquity and the early Middle Ages whose raids in Europe reached their peak in the fifth century AD and brought them into both conflicts and alliances with the Goths and other Germanic peoples. Numerous human characters in the Saga of the Volsungs are referred to as Huns, especially Atli (who is distantly based on the historical Attila the Hun) and Sigurd.

Hunding [V], a king who is killed by Helgi. His sons, including Lyngvi, kill Sigmund (1).

Hunland [V], a mythical kingdom ruled by the early Volsungs. Since Sigurd and other Volsungs are occasionally referred to as Huns, the association with that people is apparently intentional.

Hvítabǿ [R], unknown city in Europe raided by the Ragnarssons early in their career. The name would answer to *Whitby* in English, but the location does not seem to be in England.

Hvítserk [R], a son of Ragnar Lodbrók and Áslaug, sometimes called Hvítserk the Bold.

Ingibjorg [R], daughter of Eystein, who offers her in marriage to Ragnar Lodbrók.

Ívar the Boneless [R], son of Ragnar Lodbrók and Áslaug. He has no bones, according to the Saga of Ragnar Lodbrók, because his father violated his mother's warning against sleeping with her too early. In spite of his unique disability, Ívar is represented as the craftiest of his brothers, as well as something of a leader among them.

Jarizleif [V], a companion of Gunnar when he goes to Gudrún after the murder of Sigurd. The name is not Norse but appears Slavic.

Jarl [V, R], Norse title for a powerful nobleman.

Jónakr [V], a king, third husband of Gudrún and father of Hamdir, Sorli, and Erp (2).

Jormunrekk [V], a king who is promised the hand of Svanhild in marriage and later kills her by having her trampled to death by horses.

Kostbera [V], the wife of Hogni (2). She has prophetic dreams and reads runes.

Kráka [R], the name given to Áslaug by Aki and Gríma, and used by her until she reveals her true name to Ragnar when she is pregnant with Sigurd Snake-Eye. In Old Norse, the name literally means "crow."

Láganes [V], a peninsula in an unknown location, mentioned by Sinfjotli in an insult.

Langobards [V], a Germanic tribe of the early Middle Ages. They gave their name to Lombardy in Italy.

Leif [V], a captain in Helgi's navy.

Loki [V], a complicated trickster figure who helps the Norse gods in some myths and opposes them in others. In the Saga of the Volsungs, he is traveling in the company of Óðin when he kills Otter, which sets in motion the action of the remainder of the saga.

London [R], supposedly founded by Ívar according to chapter 17 of the Saga of Ragnar Loðbrók. The City of London is in fact many centuries older than the Viking Age.

Lyngvi [V], a son of Hunding who courts Hjordís in competition with Sigmund.

Munarvág [R], Old Norse name for an unknown harbor on the Danish island of Samsø.

Niflung [V], a son of Hogni (2).

Norn [V], one of the female beings who determine the fate of gods and mortals.

Norway [R], roughly coterminous with the modern country, but it is a region of small independent chiefdoms, rather than a unified nation, in the early Middle Ages.

Oddrún [V], a sister of Brynhild and Atli who is mentioned by name only once in the Saga of the Volsungs (in chapter 31), when Brynhild briefly alludes to Gunnar's secret meetings with Oddrún. This is a story told more fully in the poem *Oddrúnargrátr* (*Oddrunargratr*) in the Poetic Edda. It is also possible that Oddrún is the sister Atli is thinking of when he tells Gunnar and Hogni that they have betrayed his sister in chapter 36 of the Saga of the Volsungs.

Óðin [V, R], god of poetry and war. He is often portrayed as a shrewd figure pursuing his own selfish interests, including the dispatching of human warriors so that they may join his army in Valhalla (the "hall of the slain" where the Valkyries bring slain warriors). Óðin is very frequently seen in disguise and takes many names, but even in disguise he is usually recognizable to the reader as an old man with one eye, often dressed in a gray or blue cloak and a wide-brimmed hat.

Ogmund [R], nicknamed "the Dane." In the last chapter of the Saga of Ragnar Loðbrók, he encounters a talking wooden idol on Samsø, which claims it was made by the Ragnarssons.

Óin [V], a dwarf, father of Andvari.

Orkning [V], a warrior, brother of Kostbera.

Óskapt [V], an island mentioned by Fáfnir as the site of Ragnarok, the final battle between the gods and giants.

Otter [V], brother of Fáfnir and Regin, son of Hreidmar. He is literally an otter, and his name in Old Norse, *Otr*, is the normal Old Norse word for "otter" (and that word is used to describe him in the same chapter in which it is given as his name). He is killed by Loki, which begins the tale of the cursed treasure taken from Andvari.

Ragnar Lodbrók [R], a legendary Danish king and Viking. *Lodbrók* is not a last name but a nickname that literally means "shaggy pants" (or "shaggy chaps") and refers to the signature item of clothing that he wore when he rescued his first wife Thóra (2) from a dragon. With Thóra he is the father of Eirek and Agnar (2). After Thóra's death, he remarries to Áslaug (Kráka), and with her he is the father of Sigurd Snake-Eye, Ívar the Boneless, Hvítserk, Rognvald, and Bjorn Ironside.

Ragnarssons [R], collective designation for the sons of Ragnar Lodbrók, especially his sons with Áslaug: Sigurd Snake-Eye, Ívar the Boneless, Hvítserk, Rognvald, and Bjorn Ironside.

Ragnhild [R], mother of Harald Fairhair. She is represented as the daughter of Sigurd Snake-Eye.

Rán [V], goddess of shipwrecks and owner of a famous net that Loki borrows to catch Andvari.

Randalín [R], the name adopted by Áslaug when she accompanies her sons on their expedition to avenge Agnar (2) and Eirek, and for the remainder of her life thereafter.

Randvér [V], son of Jormunrekk, who is sent by his father to bring Svanhild to him as his bride.

Raudabjargir [V], a site where Helgi collects his troops.

Regin [V], a smith, brother of Fáfnir and Otter, and son of Hreidmar. He raises Sigurd in the kingdom of Álf (2), and reforges the sword Gram.

Rerir [V], the son of Sigi and father of Volsung.

Rhine [V], a river near the kingdom of Gjúki and his family, and the river where Gunnar and Hogni (2) hide the treasure of Fáfnir at some point after they have killed Sigurd and before they visit Atli.

Ridil [V], a sword Sigurd uses to cut open the dead dragon Fáfnir.

Rognvald [R], a son of Ragnar Loðbrók and Áslaug.

Rune [V], a letter in the alphabet used in Scandinavia before the adoption of the Roman alphabet (which is the alphabet used to write English and the Scandinavian languages today). Brynhild attributes magical properties to them in chapter 20 of the Saga of the Volsungs, in lines borrowed from the poem *Sigrdrífumál* (*Sigrdrifumal*) in the Poetic Edda.

Rus [V], a term for the people of an early medieval Swedish tribe, or the Slavic people of the kingdoms they founded in modern Russia and Ukraine. The word appears in this volume in translating Old Norse *Garðakonungr*, "king of the Rus," literally "king of *Garðaríki*," an Old Norse term for the Rus kingdoms.

Samsø [R], a small island in Denmark where Ogmund encounters a talking wooden idol that tells him it was made by the Ragnarssons. The island (known in Old Norse as *Sámsey*) seems to have had a special association with magic, as it is also mentioned as a place where Óðin practiced magic in the poem *Lokasenna* in the Poetic Edda.

Saxons [V], a Germanic tribe of the early medieval period. Anglo-Saxons (in England) or more likely, continental Saxons (in northern Germany), may be implied.

Scandinavia [V, R], used as a translation of Old Norse *Norðrlond* (literally, "Northlands"). The term refers to the countries of Norway, Denmark, and Sweden, which have closely related languages as well as strong historical links. The term often includes Iceland (which was settled from Norway), and in modern times sometimes also Finland (which has a language unrelated to Scandinavia proper, and a distinct culture, history, and mythology). It is interesting that England is included in the definition of *Norðrlond* in chapter 17 of the Saga of Ragnar Lothbrok, but throughout the early Middle Ages the English language remained very similar to its Scandinavian relatives, and the English kingdoms had frequent contact (both warlike and peaceful) with Danes and Norwegians.

Sefafjoll [V], the home of Sigrún.

Síbilja [R], a cow worshipped by Eystein in his kingdom in Sweden.

Sigar [V], briefly alluded to as a relative of Siggeir. Various medieval sources mention a Sigar in Siggeir's family, but the original relation between the two is not clear. It is unclear whether the Sigar related to Siggeir is the same as the Sigar alluded to by Guđrún in chapter 25 of the Saga of the Volsungs.

Siggeir [V], husband of Signý and killer of Volsung.

Sigi [V], a son of Óđin and father of Rerir. He is outlawed for the murder of Bređi and driven away from home.

Sigmund (1) [V], son of Volsung, brother of Signý, and father of Sinfjotli, Helgi, and Sigurđ. He is the owner of the sword later reforged as Gram, and after killing Siggeir in revenge for his father and brothers, he becomes the king of Hunland.

Sigmund (2) [V], son of Sigurđ and Guđrún.

Signý [V], daughter of Volsung, wife of Siggeir, and mother (with her brother Sigmund) of Sinfjotli.

Sigrún [V], a Valkyrie, daughter of Hogni (1), and lover of Helgi.

Sigurđ [V, R], son of Sigmund (1) and renowned for slaying Fáfnir with the sword Gram. With Brynhild, he is the father of Áslaug, and with his wife Guđrún he is the father of Svanhild and Sigmund (2).

Sigurđ Ring [R], legendary king of Denmark (who is said in other sagas to be a Swede) and father of Ragnar Lođbrók.

Sigurđ Snake-Eye [R], a son of Ragnar Lođbrók and Áslaug, named for his maternal grandfather Sigurđ and nicknamed for an eye that appears to have a snake (or dragon) in it.

Sinfjotli [V], son of Sigmund (1) and his sister Signý. He is represented as a particularly fierce warrior, thanks to his descent on both his father's and mother's side from Volsung (and therefore from Óđin).

Skađi [V], owner of the slave Bređi.

Sleipnir [V], the eight-legged stallion of Óđin, which is the father of Sigurđ's stallion Grani.

Snævar [V], a son of Hogni (2).

Sok [V], an island.

Sólar [V], a son of Hogni (2).

Sólfjoll [V], a location associated with the Volsungs.

Sorli [V], son of Guđrún and Jónakr, brother of Hamđir and Erp (2).

Southern Empire [R], a Norse designation for the Holy Roman Empire.

Spangarheiđ [R], the farm of Aki and Gríma in Norway.

Spellcaster [V], name used by Óðin in disguise in chapter 17 of the Saga of the Volsungs, and in the Poetic Edda in the poem *Reginsmál* (*Reginsmal*), which Óðin's lines in that chapter are quoted from. "Spellcaster" is a translation of Old Norse *Fjolnir*, which is of uncertain exact meaning but apparently formed from a root word that has associations with magical wisdom.

Svafrlod [V], one of Guðrún's serving-women.

Svanhild [V], daughter of Guðrún and Sigurð. She is promised in marriage to Jormunrekk and famously killed when he orders her trampled to death by horses.

Svarinshaug [V], the domain of Granmar (2).

Sveipuð [V], a stallion.

Sveggjuð [V], a stallion.

Sweden [R], in the Middle Ages, refers chiefly to the eastern part of the modern country centered around Uppsala. Much of the southern part of what is now Sweden belonged to Denmark until early modern times, and in the early medieval period Götaland was also a distinct kingdom.

Thór [V], the god of thunder and protector of humankind, who famously wields the hammer Mjollnir.

Thóra (1) [V], a friend to Guðrún during her time in Denmark after the murder of Sigurð.

Thóra (2) [R], also called Thóra Town-Doe, the first wife of Ragnar Loðbrók.

Thórð [R], one of the original settlers of Iceland, according to the Old Norse document called *Landnámabók* (Book of the Settlers). According to chapter 64 of Landnámabók, he was the great-great-grandson of Ragnar Loðbrók, and the Saga of Ragnar Loðbrók affirms the tradition of a family connection in chapter 18.

Thrasnes [V], a peninsula in an unknown location, mentioned by Granmar in an insult.

Troll [V], an evil creature of unspecified characteristics, perhaps similar to a giant but invariably ugly (whereas the giants may be attractive).

Týr [V], a one-handed god and also the name of a rune.

Uppsala [R], an important city of medieval and modern Sweden.

Valbjorg [V], an estate that is part of the inheritance of Gjúki.

Valdar [V], mentioned as a Danish companion of Gunnar, and known elsewhere as the name of a king of Denmark.

Valkyries [V], "choosers of the slain," women who fly over battlefields and conduct the spirits of the best slain warriors to Óðin in Valhalla. A Valkyrie is not a separate kind of being from humans but seems to be an occupation that mortal women (such as Sigrún and Brynhild) and even the daughters of giants (such as Hljóð) can assume.

Vanir [V], a family of gods subordinate to the Æsir and associated with agriculture, the natural world, and fertility.

Varinsey [V], an island in an unknown location, mentioned by Sinfjotli in an insult.

Varinsfjord [V], a fjord where Helgi first meets Sigrún.

Vífil [R], the ruler of Vífilsborg.

Vífilsborg [R], a city raided by the Ragnarssons in the Holy Roman Empire.

Vínbjorg [V], an estate that is part of the inheritance of Gjúki.

Vingi [V], a Hunnish messenger sent by Atli to invite Gunnar and Hogni to visit him.

Volsung [V], a famously skilled and daring warrior, the son of Rerir who is born after his mother's six-year pregnancy. He becomes king of Hunland and father of twin siblings Sigmund (1) and Signý. His descendants are known as the Volsungs in honor of him.

Volsungs [V], the name of the family descended from Volsung. Any descendant of his (e.g., Sigmund, Sigurd, Sinfjotli, Signý) can be referred to as "a Volsung."

William the Conqueror [R], the historical conqueror of and later king of England (ruled AD 1066–1087).